Stolen Secrets

By the same author

The Warrior Troll (Nightingale Books), 2007
ISBN 9781903491478

The Bogler's Apprentice (Nightingale Books), 2008
ISBN 9781903491720

Of Pipes and Potions (Nightingale Books), 2010
ISBN 9781903491935

The Quest of Snorrie Magnus (Nightingale Books), 2011
ISBN 978 1 907552 25 0

Rachael Lindsay

Stolen Secrets

Nightingale Books

NIGHTINGALE PAPERBACK

© Copyright 2013
Rachael Lindsay

A CIP catalogue record for this title is
available from the British Library.

ISBN 978 1 907552 50 2

Nightingale Books is an imprint of
Pegasus Elliot MacKenzie Publishers Ltd.
www.pegasuspublishers.com

The troll-figurine on the cover page is an original Ny-Form Troll,
www.trollsofnorway.com

First Published in 2013

Nightingale Books
Sheraton House Castle Park
Cambridge England

Printed & Bound in Great Britain

Dedication

Foor mi speshy dearigs ~ mi beebees en mi angelicors ~
Thanken, thanken foor ur lovelor.
Sonnerig, songlis, fonnerig en floweries wit u todagen
en forerver.
Kissig, kissig.

Acknowledgement

Once more, my special thanks and love to:

Sophie 'Socks' Rolland

for her fantastic artwork ~
imagination and talent, combined.

sockse@gmail.com

A note from the author ~

When I was young, I used to play in a sycamore tree at the bottom of our garden. I knew each sturdy branch and gnarled whirl of its bark; the tree's own fingerprints.

It was always best in summer. I climbed a rope ladder into my imagination and disappeared amongst the tree's leafy robes. I clasped it so hard, its imprint stayed upon my cheek and green stained my white socks.

In that tree, I rode the ocean's storms.

In that tree, I could fly, swoop and soar.

In that tree, I fought pirates and tamed dragons.

It was my special place, that tree.

My secret world…

Contents

Troll-Talk ~ A Glossary

A

angelicor – angel
animor(es) – animal(s)
askli – ask/to ask

B

backen – back
badli – bad
beebee – baby
beetloosh – beetle
biggy – big
borg – bye
brekenfasht – breakfast
bringor – bring/to bring
brokisht – broken
bookor – book
butteri-fleegen – butterflies
buzzor(s) – bee(s)

C

carefloosh – careful
chattoori – to chat/to talk/chatting
clinkoori – to clink glasses ("cheers!")
cloudoosh – cloud(s)
comli – come/coming/to come
creepori – creep/to creep/creepy

D

dearig(s) – dear one(s)
dedden – deadly/dangerous
dee – the
dingle-donglor – bell
dis – this
doctoori – doctor
drinkoosh – drink

E

eatig – eat/to eat
eggsie(s) – egg(s)
en – and
es – is/are/it's
excitig – exciting

F

fastli – quickly/fast
fatli – fat
feelen – feel/to feel
fetchen – fetch/to fetch
findor – find/to find
fishen – fish
flaggermuss(es) – bat(s)
floweri(es) – flower(s)
fonnerig – fun
forerver – forever
foresh – forest
foor – for
frendor(s) – friend(s)

G

gib – give/to give
goingor – going/to go
gooshty – good

H

hab – have/to have
halloo – hello
happenig – happened/happening
happli – happy
heer – here
helpen – help/to help

Herbie Poshtig – collecting pouch (usually for herbs)
homerig – home/house
honig – honey
hurtig – hurt/to hurt

I

im – I/I'm

J

K

kissig(s) – kiss(es)
krankoosh – ill/poorly

L

laterig – late
leftig – left/to leave
leggor(s) – leg(s)
liker – like
littelor – little
lovelor – love/to love

M

marvellurg – marvellous
mattoori – (the) matter
meer – me
mekken – make/to make
menor – people/men
mi – my
mistig – misty
Mistig Vorter – Misty Water (Thom's boat)
monkee-monkee – monkey business
moonish – moon
morgy – morning
morish – more
morsi(es) – mouse (mice)
mushroomer – mushrooms
musten – must

N

nachtor – night
nay – no
needen – needing/need/to need
nestli(es) – nest(s)
nettli(es) – nettle(s)
nics – not
notoori(s) – note(s)

O

oon – one
oop – up
oor – our
oos – us
outen – outside/out of

P

pictoori(s) – picture(s)
pleasor – please
problemori(s) – problem(s)
pussor – cat
pyor – pie

Q

R

runnig – run/to run

S

sadli – sad
saftoosh – safe/safely
scent-pretti(es) – perfume(s)
secresht – secret

shineror – shine/to shine
shleepish – sleepy
shoo-shoo – go away
shtay – stay
shtop – stop
sistoori – sister
sitli – sit/to sit
songli – song
sonnerig – sunshine
soonig – soon
soundor – sound/noise
speshy – special
strangeror – strange
strikor – strike/to strike
strongish – strong

$\mathcal{T}$

tay – tea
thanken – thank you
thinken – think/thinking/to think
thingor(s) – thing(s)
thri – three
todagen – today
tweetors – birds
tvo – two/too/to

$\mathcal{U}$

u – you
udder – other
ur – your
urnli – only

$\mathcal{V}$

varken – (to) wake
ve – we
veg – way
verisht – very
vi – why
vildi – wild
vorter – water

$\mathcal{W}$

wass – what's/what
wisperoo – wispy
wit – with

$\mathcal{X}$

$\mathcal{Y}$

yo – yes

$\mathcal{Z}$

Chapter One

"My home is my nest. My nest is my home."

The night owls have swooped soundlessly to their beds, feathers fluffed and fresh with forest air. The bats have quick-flitted to their roosts, to dangle and swing. The dark, dark creatures have scuttled into their hidey-holes.

Shhh…

All is secret-silent in the forest.

The hedgehogs are tucked up, embraced tightly in leafy curls. The foxes have long since reached the snug safety of their dens.

Shhh…

All is still.

Sleep hangs heavy in the air, awaiting the dawn.

This is the magical moment when night meets day; a pause, as night ceases and the sky softens.

A pale finger of light points to a great ramshackle gathering of twigs and sticks, feathers and moss; a magnificent magpie jumble of collected bird-bedding scraps, high up in a tree. A rope bridge links this nest, precariously, to the nearest sturdy branch of a neighbouring pine. A worn, rickety-pickety ladder leads down to the forest floor.

Finnr, the tree-troll, stirs.

A snuffle. A rub of the nose.

The gentle light arrives at the entrance to his home. A fresh day! Dewy brightness to welcome into the forest!

With a clearing *harrumph* of his throat, a yawn and a stretch, Finnr fastens the buttons on his dungarees and collects his green, floppy hat from a twig hook. He climbs out through the nest-hole and breathes in the pine-scented air, with eyes closed, better to savour the moment. Then, with hat now covering balding head, white whiskers protruding from underneath, the tree-troll tap-taps his weather-stick and addresses the birds nesting around him.

"Gooshty morgy, mi littelor tweetors! Dee morgy songli, pleasor!"

Hearing familiar troll-talk, tiny waking chirrups ensue, bird-nudgings and shufflings, blinks and chatters.

A few more taps; a dramatic pause, as Finnr raises his hands to conduct:

"Oon! Tvo! Thri!"

In wonderful unison, the dawn chorus begins.

&

This was how every day began for Finnr.

He had lived in his special tree house for countless years, adding to its nest structure, season on season. His many bird companions lodged with him, and came and went with the passing of time. The old troll had known generation after generation of fat wood pigeons, pied flycatchers and tree

24

pipits. He had shared his nest-home with turtle doves and cuckoos, wood larks and waxwings. He had families of needletails close by in the hollow trunks and he knew all the woodpeckers' mothers, fathers, sisters, brothers, nieces, nephews and cousins. He even had tawny owls waking at night and silently taking flight from their tree holes, returning later with their supper.

Every morning, Finnr would rise before the forest itself had woken. Every morning, he would tap-tap his weather-stick. Every morning, he would conduct the dawn chorus.

The birdsong floated this morning, like every other, through the wakening woodland, encouraging others to join in; the tweets, chirrups, chirps, peeps and twitters swelling into a musical refrain which no living creature could ignore. At the sound, other forest trolls awoke, stretching and yawning, smiling and blinking, all happy to live in their secret homes, tucked away from the Big People. Hildi cut bread and spooned out bilberries for breakfast. Thom collected his bucket of fjord water and let Grimo out to stretch his paws. Dotta warmed goat's milk over her fire, humming and swaying, as Grimhildr stacked the wood. Hairy Bogley and Ulf heard the birds but knew it was their signal to sleep on, in their smoky home-cave above the fjord, tired from their night-time gatherings.

With bare, hairy feet, Finnr stepped onto his rope bridge and pointed his weather-stick up at the sky. He nodded in satisfaction, his troll-tail swishing slightly.

"Sonnerig wit wisperoo cloudoosh," he murmured. "Verisht gooshty, gooshty." It was going to be a perfect day for tending to his flowers. The tree-troll turned back to look at his home and he drew in a breath of satisfaction and great pleasure. The seedlings he had planted on the outside had flourished over the last few weeks and bright colours sprouted from every tiny, mossy nook. It was a glorious, hanging, flower basket of a tree house nest.

Finnr loved it.

The birds loved it.

The bees and the butterflies loved it.

The trolls, who gathered mushrooms and firewood from the forest floor below, loved it.

The flowers were not just for decoration and everyone's delight, though. They were not just for scenting the forest air, mingling with pine and herbs, encouraging nectar sipping insects and pollen collecting honey-makers. Finnr collected their petals for perfumes and fragrant pomander making. He knew exactly which, and how many, to mix together for the perfect aroma bouquet, and he knew at what time to gather the flowers' softness into his bottles and jars. His skill in choosing and blending was unique. No other troll had his knowledge.

Finnr also knew everything about bark and leaves, seeds and roots, and deep-buried truffles. He knew how to forage without upsetting the delicate balance of the woods. He did not disturb the beetles and spiders, or the many-legged millipedes, if he could help it. He knew how to dry pieces of fallen bark, later grinding them between two specially chosen stones into a fine powder. He knew how to boil gnarled roots in collected waterfall splashes, over his little fire in a clearing, enjoying the earthy bonfire smell. With age-old knowledge, he cooled and bottled the liquor, ready for use when necessary.

Finnr was always busy.

For Finnr had a gift.

He was able to select exactly the right powder to mix with milk or water, to pour exactly the right amount of root liquor and to combine any number of different ingredients to make all manner of concoctions.

In short, he was a medicine-maker.

There was a certain magic about him, which enabled him to understand a fever or a condition or an illness, and then to blend his home-made forest remedies for immediate recovery of the patient. All trolls have some knowledge of medicines; Hildi was very skilled in honey medicine-making and Dotta tended her animals with fearful jumbles of love and hope, but Finnr was the real expert.

He kept his pots and jars and bottles in small, feather-lined hollows in his tree-nest, winched up in a small bucket, by rope, from the ground below. At times, he had barely enough room to curl up inside, if he had been particularly busy with his alchemy that day. Somehow though, there would be just a little space left for Finnr to lie on the downy floor, with hairy troll-knees tucked up underneath his soft blanket and there he would sleep soundly, until it was time to rouse his bird lodgers.

§

All Finnr's birds were wild. They chose to share his nest-home because they felt safe and there were always scraps of food available. They were free to fly away and nest elsewhere,

27

should they wish to, and so they came and went of their own free will. However, whilst Finnr loved them all and enjoyed their company, he longed for a *special* friend. After all, Hildi and Thom had each other, Grimo the cat and Tracker the dog, not to mention their mice. Dotta and Grimhildr had their flaggermusses, Pipi and Fug. Hairy Bogley lived with Ulf and even Snorrie Magnus had Herpet, the frog. Finnr had hoped a little hedgehog he came across one day would adopt him, but getting a hedgehog up and down the tree had proved tricky and it was far kinder to leave him snuffling for worms amongst the leaves.

So, it was with some concern, but also a certain degree of excitement one day, that he found a lost egg. There was no evidence of the nest from which it had come. The parents were not calling for it. They were nowhere to be seen. Luckily it was still perfect; smooth, glossy and olive-brown.

And still warm.

Finnr picked it up from the moss which had cushioned it, turned it over tenderly in his knobbly fingers and then popped it under his hat. It made him smile - an egg on an egg-head! He made haste back to his tree, carefully climbing his rickety-pickety ladder to the rope bridge, hoping and hoping that the egg would survive. For fourteen vigilant troll-dawns, Finnr kept his hat on his head. He slept upright, as best he could, so his hat-incubator would stay in place, snugly cosseting the precious contents. Occasionally, he would roll his head gently on his shoulders, to turn the egg as a mother bird would, in the nest. When his head itched, he did *not* scratch.

Then, as Finnr was walking in the woods one fine morning, he felt a slight movement under his hat. He stood stock still, holding his breath, waiting.

Could it be?

Yes! There it was again!

Without doubt, the egg was twitching slightly. Its smooth shell was moving against his own bald crown!

Finnr looked around for a comfortable spot to sit down and quickly espied a risen tree root, covered in fallen pine needles. He lowered himself down, keeping his back and head poker-straight, and cautiously removed the soft, floppy hat for the first time in two weeks, carefully rolling the egg into it. A delightful rush of cool air freshened his head. Holding the hat in both hands, he peered in. There was the egg, nestled cosily – with a definite, fine, hairline crack beginning to show.

"Yo, yo!" Finnr exclaimed in joy. "Mi beebee tweetor comli! Mi littelor eggsie es brokisht!"

The new father-to-be looked around him excitedly, hoping he could share his news with another forest troll, but he was quite alone. A scritch-scratching sound was to be heard, delicate but insistent. Finnr stared wide-eyed into the depths of his hat.

"Comli, comli, mi beebee," he encouraged, urging the tiny beak to peck and the little toes to scrape.

The crack became a chink. As Finnr watched, a flimsy, white tissue layer was revealed and he could see fidgety movement underneath it. His heart began to pound. A brand new life! Here in his hands!

He had seen many baby birds in the lodging nests of his home, but the hatchings had always been quiet, private moments for the mother and father; the wise troll left them to their wild nature and instincts. This though, was different. This was a hatching of his own making!

He, Finnr, had found and adopted this egg, so full of promise.

He, Finnr, had cared for it and kept it warm, day and night.

He, Finnr, was responsible for maintaining the little life which was erupting in his very own hat!

His heart swelled with pride.

And so, after much wriggling and chipping, scratching and scraping, when the damp fledgling head finally poked out of the shell, the first thing the baby nightingale saw was Finnr's beaming face!

She saw his bright, beady, bird-like eyes.

She saw his long, poky beak-like nose.

She saw his happy, gappy-toothed grin.

It was love at first sight!

"Halloo mi beebee," whispered the tree-troll, watching the bird put her head on one side to consider him. "Im lovelor u! U shtay wit meer? Pleasor?"

Grimhildr and Dotta were firm when Finnr asked for their advice. The two sister-trolls were used to looking after wild animals which they rescued from danger in the forest, and they certainly knew the heartache of letting them return. They knew it would be wrong for Finnr to try to keep the baby bird as a pet. He could feed her, like her parents would have done, but when the time came for the nightingale to fly from Finnr's nest, he must let her go free.

"It was love at first sight."

Finnr knew they were right. If the little bird chose to stay that would be wonderful, but if she chose to fly off into her own life, so be it. So, lovingly, he cared for the bird, which he named Luscinia, feeding her on ants and chewy little grubs and insects until she was big enough to find her own. He understood her tweets, her songs, her chatter. He delighted in her plain brown feathers and dull appearance, thinking her quite the most perfect little bird he had ever seen. He listened, enthralled, as Luscinia found her adult voice. On still, late summer evenings, the nightingale would sit perched on Finnr's toes and entertain all who could hear her, with the most melodious of birdsongs. Her warbles and whistles echoed through the night-time wood, when all other birds were quiet. She had a captive, and captivated, audience.

Luscinia chose to stay.

The dawn chorus finished as the sun rose to settle amongst wispy summer clouds. In a clearing in the forest, Finnr busied himself with a small cooking fire and stirred some sticky porridge in his old pot. He was just about to sit down and eat when he heard his name being called. Looking up, he saw his good friend Thom striding towards him, Tracker at his heels. A small jar was swinging from a loop on Thom's green dungarees and a clutch of dried nettles was in his hairy troll-hand.

"Halloo Thom! Comli en eatig brekenfasht wit meer," greeted Finnr, waving his wooden spoon over his head, blobs of porridge dripping from it.

"Yo, yo! Thanken, thanken!" Thom grinned, taking his place by the smoking fire and patting the ground to show Tracker where to sit. He had already eaten, but it would have been impolite to refuse the usual troll hospitality. "Im bringor gooshty buzzor honig en nettlies foor tay, Finnr," he continued. "Hildi 'shoo-shoo' meer todagen – Hildi mekken pictooris foor Biggy Menor dis morgy."

Finnr nodded in understanding and they sat in smoky, companionable silence as the tree-troll stirred the contents of his pot. Sometimes it was good to be like this, just the two of them, in the forest, Thom away from his beloved troll-lady, doing man-stuff with Finnr. Sometimes, Hildi wanted their little home to herself, so she could spend some happy hours making her pictures. She used them in exchange for items the trolls could not find or make for themselves, although any dealings with the Big People always carried an element of risk. She had a few special contacts in the nearby town; Big People who would accept her as she was, not jeer at her short, hairy legs and trollish ways; Big People who would not want to disturb their way of life, or capture them to use as workers, or do them harm. These few Big People valued Hildi's creative pieces and would sell them on, without telling others who had made them. Thom knew better than to get in her way once she had cleared the tiny kitchen table and begun to arrange her herbs and ferns and dried forest flowers.

As always, Finnr welcomed the company. He accepted Thom's honey with enthusiasm and spooned a dollop into his porridge. Then, he scrambled up his ladder and returned, swinging from his tree house like a monkey, with two wooden bowls he had fashioned recently from fallen pine. Thom replaced the cooking pot with another, filled with water this time, dousing the nettles, letting them heat and stew.

Contentedly listening to the crackle of the burning sticks, wafting the smoke away from their faces now and then, the two friends tucked their troll-tails underneath them and shared the sweet, steaming oats.

What a perfect start to the day!

After breakfast there would be jobs to do, but ones which would be fun and not a hardship. The flowers in Finnr's tree house would be watered and picked. The bees and insects would join him as he preened and tweaked. Perhaps he would wander, weather-stick in hand, through the green forest, collecting bark and roots. Perhaps he would join Thom in his little blue fishing boat, Mistig Vorter, out on the fjord, letting his hands trail in the icy water.

What a wonderful life!

Nothing could spoil it.

Then, unexpectedly, a cloud shifted to block the sun. The trolls felt a cool breath of wind, which made the backs of their hairy necks goose-pimple, momentarily.

Finnr looked up at the sky, quizzically.

He raised a wise eyebrow and then a frown creased his face. He was good at reading nature. He was good at understanding signs. He had not expected the weather to change this morning.

He felt ever so slightly uneasy.

The day had started off so cheerily…

Here he was with his good friend, eating good food. All was well in the forest as far as he could tell. The birds and woodland creatures were fine and dandy. The sunshine had been so bright.

One, dark, rain cloud.

Was this a sign?

Chapter Two

"Ideas for my notebook. My notebook for ideas."

The rain, now falling in the forest, also pattered on the roof of a certain Big Man's house. It ran in rivulets to the gutters and down the pipes, into the litter-blocked drains on the street. It gave the dirty windows the only wash they ever had, but still left them streaked and grimy.

Waking rather late in the morning, Doctor Klumpet rolled out of the wrong side of bed and spread his fat, pink feet on the thick rug. He fumbled around on the chest of drawers for his glasses, his pudgy fingers groping blindly, sending a stack of coins spinning onto the floor. His notebook fell with them, loose pages of money calculations scattering in disarray.

"SCARAB!" he boomed. "WHERE ARE YOU?"

The effort made him wheeze and for several seconds, he could not take a breath until a thick, sticky cough had spluttered from his mouth. Recovering with some difficulty, he thundered again.

"MISTER SCARAB! COME HERE, DIRECTLY!"

There was a light skittering sound of quick feet on cold, stone steps, and the door was opened wide.

"About time too!" Doctor Klumpet grumbled, looking at his scrawny assistant. "What took you so long?"

"Sorry, sorry, Doctor K!" came the soft, breathy reply. "I have things to do, you know! I was busy, busy packing your bag up for the day. I think we might need some more leeches before long, and your Wonderful Wheel of Medicine Magnificus needs oily-oiling."

"Never mind the leeches and the Wonderful Wheel of Medicine Magnificus Mister Scarab, did you pack my toffees?" asked the doctor. "You know I can't work without them."

"Yes, yes, Doctor K! I would never, ever forget your toffee-toffees!"

"Good man! I have to have my *carrrrrramels…*" the doctor salivated, rolling the *rrrr* with his tongue, as if he did indeed already have a mouthful. "Beautiful butterscotch balls of *crrrrrreamy* gorgeousness!"

Mister Scarab smiled a pale, sickly smile and clasped his hands together. His bony knuckles became quite white. He knew when to keep quiet and this was one of those moments. He let the doctor enjoy the thought of sweet toffees to come and waited, patiently. He stood before his employer, rather stooped and a little shrivelled, with a fawning expression but sharp, clever eyes. He had been employed by Klumpet for the last ten years and was used to his ways. Although he was a miserable-looking specimen, he thoroughly enjoyed his work. It gave him a sense of importance he would not have had elsewhere, since he was Klumpet's right hand man and as such, held in high regard in the town. He earned a good wage from the doctor's profits and the two were united in their avaricious determination to create as much wealth as possible.

37

Scarab had ambitious dreams of owning a huge mansion one day and of spending his retirement relaxing on the doctor's yacht, as they sailed warm, exotic waters. Perhaps they would explore desert islands with swaying palm trees, catch delicious fish in shimmering nets and cook them on the beach as the sun set. Perhaps they would have their own crew to toil away at the ropes and sails, whilst others served them fancy drinks and sweetmeats from silver platters. Oh what bliss! He spent many hours in bed at night, fidgeting and scheming, twitching, planning and preparing for the future. He had to keep on the right side of the doctor; he needed Klumpet's knowledge of medicine. In return, Klumpet acknowledged that Mister Scarab was essential for new ideas and full-time assistance.

They were a money-making dream-team.

The exorbitant fees they charged for visits to homes of the Big People in the town were paid, because there was no choice. Doctor Klumpet was the only practitioner of medicine for miles around and Mister Scarab's idea of making house calls to see his patients, instead of running a costly surgery, meant he could charge more. In fact, he could charge whatever he liked and put his fees up at a moment's notice. It was an excellent business!

"We already have many, many house calls lined up for today, Doctor K," Mister Scarab continued, passing a silk dressing gown to cover his employer's faded, blue-striped pyjamas, the buttons straining against his round belly.

Doctor Klumpet belched as he reached for a large, gold, signet ring, forcing it over a swollen knuckle.

"Better put extra toffees in, then!"

38

The sudden rain had sent Thom on his way, Tracker at his heels. It had fallen in heavy drops onto the fire, making it hiss and sending more smoke into the forest. Finnr stamped on the embers in his bare feet, making sure no risky spark remained, then hurried up his rickety-pickety ladder to the rope bridge and into his nest-home. He shrugged off his surprise at the change in the sky. Maybe his weather-stick just got it wrong today. There was no need for concern; everything was fine. He took off his hat and hung it up, whistling as he did so. Then he sat on his haunches, snug and warm, listening to the pitter-patter of the rain as it landed on branches, twigs, leaves and pine needles. There would be no need to water the flowers *this* morning! The butterflies had disappeared hurriedly from nectar-laden larders where they had been sipping. The birds had become quiet and still.

Luscinia however, never far away, responded to Finnr's whistling and rustled through the thicket of the nest to join him.

"Comli, comli mi lovelor Luscinia," the tree-troll beckoned, tenderly. "Sitli en shtay wit meer. Im mekken notooris in mi speshy bookor."

So saying, Finnr turned to one of the many storage nest-holes set into the soft lining of his home and rummaged around. Out came two stubby pieces of charcoal and an old, leather-bound notebook. The nightingale took up her perch on

39

Finnr's grubby toes and watched him turn the book over in his hands.

How precious this notebook was!

Finnr grinned as he held it to his nose so he could take a deep breath in and smell the cover. He stroked it lovingly and gave a contented sigh. This was his most valuable possession! He remembered the day that Hairy Bogley, the hermit troll, had arrived with it for him. He had not asked where it had come from; Hairy would not have told him. All trolls lived simple lives and, although they had many things of importance to *them*, they rarely had any item of actual costly value. They regarded as essential only love and friendship, the natural world of animals and plants, cool water and fresh air. They shunned the ways of the Big People and their greedy fixation with money. It had no meaning for them and they did not understand it.

Finnr had needed a notebook though and, over the years, it had become very special to him. It was full of memories and so, irreplaceable. He opened it with care and turned each ivory parchment page. There before him, was a lifetime's work, meticulously recorded by feather quill dipped in blackberry juice, from rough charcoal notes and work-in-progress scribblings. There were medicines and remedies drawn in detailed pictures, together with samples of roots, pressed berries, bark, leaves and seeds. Tallies were documented during mixing sessions, to be written up more formally later on, showing number of pinches of *this*, or dried leaves of *that*, or tiny drops of *the other*. Some were ancient cures passed down from forefathers; whispered, explained, taught. Some were Finnr's own ideas using an acquired skill, technique or new ingredient. Some were modifications and improvements of old methods, tested by Finnr, who had a particular talent for that sort of thing. It was a precious keepsake of troll-secrets and information; a compilation of many years' work and innate, natural troll knowledge. The old tree-troll was part-historian and part-scientist – and *very* sentimental. He had to keep this notebook safe because he could no longer remember all the information it held. It was far better, now he was this age, to record every detail for easy reference and for other, future medicine-troll use.

Finnr picked up his charcoal as Luscinia began to preen her feathers. A soothing flower balm for blistered ember-feet was needed.

ဆာ

Mister Scarab scuttled ahead of Doctor Klumpet, carrying the medical bag and a sheet of paper with names and addresses on. Big, fat plops of rain were making the list rather soggy, but the assistant could remember who needed to be seen and carried it only to appear important, busy and bustling. The doctor lumbered behind, panting, umbrella in hand, cursing the weather. More than once, he had been squinting ahead instead of looking down at his feet and as a result, the hems of his loud, checked trousers were wet-through with puddle-splashings. By the time they had reached the first house, he was red-faced and beads of sweat had broken out on his brow.

"...the hems of his loud, checked trousers were wet-through..."

"Not s-so f-fast, Scarab!" he puffed as they paused before knocking. "Why-why do you s-scurry off s-so quickly?" Dropping the umbrella, he bent over double, with hands on knees, to catch his breath.

"Beetle by name, beetle by nature, Doctor K! You know that!" answered the assistant, spitting on one thin hand and smoothing his lanky hair across his head. "We have much to do today, as you know. We really can't dawdle!"

So saying, he straightened the collar of his bottle-green overcoat, shiny with the wet, and rat-tatted at the door. He made a quick gesture to indicate Klumpet should wipe the corner of his mouth, as a fleck of white spittle needed to be removed, and then he stood to one side to allow the doctor to enter first…

Five short minutes later, the pair was once more standing on the street. Mister Scarab weaseled a wad of cash deftly into the inside pocket of his overcoat, as the doctor rubbed his hands together. Klumpet blinked his watery eyes quickly as he licked his moist, sausage lips in excitement.

"An excellent start to the day, Scarab! Excellent!"

"Not sure we needed *both* the leeches, Doctor K. They don't grow on trees, you know! They are getting more and more difficult to get hold of these days."

"Nonsense!" came the retort. "I'm the doctor, so just remember your place! You, Scarab, are merely my minion – my underling – my gofer. You might have some good business sense, but I *know* medical facts! I wanted to use both leeches: one for each eyelid. Bound to help the old lady to see better!

These ancient methods are tried and trusted, believe me. There's no need for new-fangled prescriptions for pills and tablets! Just rely on my old-fashioned, no-nonsense approach. I know what people want – and of course, I want people to *think* they are getting value for money!" He chuckled suddenly, behind one plump hand. "Even if they aren't!"

Mister Scarab smirked, nodded in agreement and ticked the name from his list. He cast a glance at the doctor who was busy stuffing a fat toffee into his mouth. It was a good job he was very convincing when he was with the patients, Scarab thought, because right now he looked like an overgrown schoolboy. At least the rain had finally stopped so they could make better progress. Mister Scarab shook out the umbrella and folded it into precise pleats, then he took hold of Klumpet's elbow in order to guide him.

"Onwards, up the street, Doctor K! People to see. Money to make!"

Finnr had finished his notes and with a chuff-chuff under the nightingale's beak, he got to his feet. Luscinia fluttered softly onto the feather covered floor and watched as the troll tidied his writing away, into its little hole inside the nest. The notebook fitted there perfectly, with charcoal sticks and feather quill on the top, ready for another day. Finnr was very fussy about keeping neat and as uncluttered as possible, because space was limited and he liked everything to be in its proper place.

"Luscinia, mi speshy tweetor," Finnr said, gently. "Im mekken scent-pretties todagen. Im needen floweries foor dee butteri-fleegen."

Luscinia nodded her grey-brown head and sang a note or two in approval. Finnr whistled the notes back to her and she took her leave of the nest-home, chack-chacking happily as she flew. The little bird knew which flowers Finnr would need for his perfumes today. They had tried and tested a few combinations recently and all they were missing were wild rose and lavender. Those would be easy to collect!

Whilst his little helper was gone, Finnr took a small bottle from a nest-hole. It had a tiny glass stopper which caught the light and sent rainbow-spangles across his face. It contained the mustard-yellow oil of jonquil, and gave a sudden burst of fresh, spring fragrance when the stopper was removed. It had the ability to transport the mind to warm meadows and sunshine, for a fleeting, calming moment or two. Finnr knew it well and, with skilful blending of rose and lavender, would be able to make a beautiful fragrance, perfect for dabbing onto his butterflies' wings! The butterflies would then flit through the forest, spreading the scent, encouraging birds and insects to visit flowers. The following pollination would create more flowers and seeds for Finnr's medicine storage, next year.

The thought *usually* made Finnr smile in satisfaction. Today though, he had a nagging doubt. It was all very well, this gathering, mixing, bottling and shaking, but what of it *then*? His nest-home was getting full of jars and bottles and samples and testers. He had some from years before, tucked away and not yet used. Not tried. Not tested. He was frustrated that his remedies were not given the chance to restore good health.

Another thought occurred to him as he began to count how many medicines he had stored. What was the use of his notebook? His marvellous compendium of ideas? His treasured collection of notes about bark and leaves? His detailed anthology and catalogue of seeds, berries and roots? If the medicines were not to be used, why write their recipes down at all?

Finnr shook his head. Why indeed?

Were all his efforts to be in vain?

His problem was plain to see: trolls were too healthy! This was, of course a good thing; Finnr would be the first to say how wonderful this was. The forest trolls, the mountain trolls and those who lived by the water's edge were all as fit as fleas. They ate well, from nature's cupboards. They kept themselves busy and active, going about their daily lives in both work and play – chopping and gathering firewood, swimming in the bracing water of the fjords, rowing boats, climbing trees and exploring their troll-world. They breathed either the fresh mountain air, or that of the sea. They had few worries and slept well at night. In short, they lived long, happy, healthy lives.

That gave Finnr, the medicine-maker, few opportunities to practise his skills and use his talents to the full.

For the second time that day, a cloud seemed to appear in Finnr's world. It was most unusual for him to feel like this.

When Luscinia returned with a beak full of flower stems and petals, even her bright eyes did not cheer him.

"Ah, Luscinia," Finnr sighed, stroking her back absent-mindedly with one charcoal-stained finger. "Cloudoosh es wit meer." He made a sad face and his little friend, having dropped her flowers, flapped up to his shoulder. "Mi bookor wit notooris es nay gooshty. Trolls es strongish en happli!" He gestured to all his jars, bottles of remedies and collected ingredients, with his weather-stick. "Puh!"

Luscinia, as always, understood. The two of them had a way of communicating which was unique to them. Finnr understood her song; the nightingale understood his whistles. Finnr understood her fluttering and chat-chats; Luscinia understood his muttering and troll-chat. The two regarded each other for a moment, lost in thought, and then the bird gave a series of sudden trills! *An idea!*

In a flurry of feathers, she flew from Finnr's shoulder to the nest-hole and peeped out. Another trill and then a returning flit, to whistle and warble with enthusiasm, her song filling the cosy home and causing quite a stir amongst the other birds.

Finnr's eyes widened in excitement! What a wonderful plan! It was a bit daring – and he would have to take care – but the thrill of being able to use his medicines and methods at last, outweighed any thought of danger!

"Yo, yo, Luscinia!" Finnr cried. "U comli wit meer?"

The nightingale had already plucked the green, floppy hat from its twig hook and let it fall at his bare, hairy troll-feet. Try leaving her behind! Finnr scooped it up. He grinned his best gappy-toothed grin and began to gather a few special medicines. Into the hat they went, with his tiny bottle of jonquil oil, stopper firmly in place. He jammed the hat onto his head and grabbed his notebook, not caring for once that the quill and charcoal sticks scattered onto the floor. Clutching his weather-stick in eagerness, he made haste to his rope bridge.

"Gooshty borg mi littelor tweetors!" he called out as he swang down his rickety-pickety ladder to the forest floor. "Im goingor mekken excitig thingors! Comli, Luscinia, comli!"

Why hadn't he thought of this before? So many different Big People out there! All ages, sizes and shapes!

Finnr, the medicine-maker was coming!

Chapter Three

"Fools and money. Money and fools."

"At last you're here, doctor! What *am* I going to do? My insides ache *so* badly. I can't eat or drink or sleep for the pain and..." There was a slight hesitation. "...I haven't been to the toilet for *days*!"

Doctor Klumpet regarded his groaning patient without the slightest flicker of sympathy. After a moment of silent reflection, he stretched out a pink palm towards his assistant, as if he were a surgeon requesting his scalpel. Mister Scarab obliged by rooting about in the medical supplies bag. He unpacked scissors, bandages and plasters. He rummaged around the jars of leeches and the oiled Wonderful Wheel of Medicine Magnificus, to locate the needles and syringes which he set out on a grubby piece of grey muslin. Finally he found what the doctor needed and popped a specially unwrapped toffee onto the doctor's moist hand. The room was filled with the slurping, sticky sound of Klumpet's chewing. He sucked the sweet, buttery juices through his teeth, drooling slightly, and then swallowed with a rather large gulp.

His patient didn't notice. He was too consumed with misery. He rolled his eyes in his head as he grasped his middle, bent over double in agony.

"I feel *so* ill," he moaned. "Please help me, doctor! I'm a desperate man!"

Doctor Klumpet took in a deep breath and glanced at a clock on the wall. Had he been five minutes yet? He liked to make sure he spent a full five minutes with each person; it was only fair. How else could he charge his costly fees?

"Scarab," he announced solemnly at last, "the Wonderful Wheel of Medicine Magnificus, if you please."

"And a bottle of gloopy-poop-poop?"

"And a bottle of gloopy-poop-poop. Nothing else for it, I'm afraid."

At the doctor's grave face, the patient began to sob. This was sounding so serious! Whatever was going to happen to him? He clutched at his belly and began to rock backwards and forwards, holding his breath. Thank goodness the clever doctor was here with him! Surely soon he would get some relief from this torment.

The Wonderful Wheel of Medicine Magnificus was brought forward and placed with great ceremony in front of Doctor Klumpet. A small bottle of white viscous liquid was unstoppered and placed at its side. Mister Scarab awaited instructions. He assumed a sombre facial expression, befitting the occasion and tried very hard not to count each greedy minute that passed by. His behaviour was all part of the act, the show, the Pantomime of Pretence. The more they could fool people, the better, and the two of them were very skilled at doing so.

The Wonderful Wheel of Medicine Magnificus was in fact, a child's colour wheel. An artist's simple tool. It was made from plastic and divided into equal triangles of bright primary yellow, red and blue, together with secondary orange, purple and green. When the doctor licked one podgy finger and flicked the wheel it twizzled on a tiny point at its centre, blending the colours in a dizzying blur. As it was spinning, Klumpet placed a calming hand, flat on the sweating brow of his patient and closed his eyes. All that could be heard was the slight rhythmic humming of the wheel as it spun around – and around – and around.

Whir – whir – whir!

After a few tension-filled seconds, the doctor raised another finger in the air. Enjoying the drama of the moment he paused, checking all around were paying full attention to his expertise and skill. Seeing that the unfortunate patient and Scarab were focused entirely on him, he brought his finger down onto the wheel with a heavy prod, causing it to come to a sudden, skidding halt. Doctor Klumpet peered through his glasses at the triangle he had selected.

"Hmmm… thought as much!" he declared, casting a glance at the patient's anxious face. "Your brightest orange, if you please Mister Scarab. I think five drops of the elixir in the gloopy-poop-poop should do the trick."

With great seriousness, Scarab searched once more in the medical bag and withdrew a small phial of orange food colouring. He squeezed the pipette gently and sucked up a few drops. He plopped them with great importance and aplomb, one at a time, into the bottle of white gloop.

Plop! Plop! Plop! Plop! Plop!

The orange droplets sank slowly to the bottom and formed a thin layer. The bottle was lifted and the opening covered with one bony thumb. The assistant shook it vigorously before handing it over.

"Your Medicine Magnificus, Doctor Klumpet, made with precision and to perfection!"

"As always, Mister Scarab. I would expect nothing less," came the reply. "Hold the patient's nose, if you will."

Before the unfortunate man knew what was happening, his nose was firmly pinched and his head jerked backwards. The doctor placed a fat thumb on the patient's chin and forced open his mouth. The gloopy-poop-poop was unceremoniously poured down his throat. His mouth was then clamped shut to force him to swallow. Gagging and spluttering, the man waved his arms wildly in the air, attempting to escape this sudden onslaught and by the time the pair had let go, his chair had slipped from beneath him and he had ended up on the floor in a dribbly, sticky, orange medicine sort of mess.

Doctor Klumpet smacked his hands together in satisfaction.

"All over!" he announced. "Job done! Money, please."

The poor sufferer coughed and retched as he struggled to fumble for the cash in a tatty wallet. His ashen face had now taken on an alarming purple hue and great blue veins stood out in his neck. He handed his payment over to Scarab, one hand still clutching his middle.

"When will I feel better, Doctor Klumpet?" he gasped.

"All in good time, Mister Colic. All in good time."

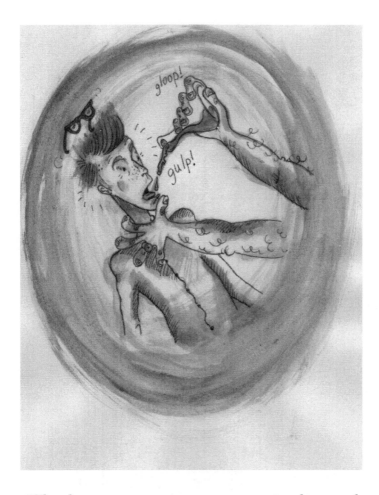

"The gloopy-poop-poop was unceremoniously poured down his throat."

Without a sideways glance, or any concern at all, Mister Scarab stuffed the money into his overcoat pocket and began to pack the medical supplies bag once more. In went the scissors, bandages and plasters. With due reverence, he placed the Wonderful Wheel of Medicine Magnificus on top. In went the needles and syringes and the grubby piece of grey muslin.

The doctor cleared his throat.

"Have you forgotten something, Scarab?"

Mister Scarab looked about him and seeing all was packed away looked a little nonplussed. The patient looked pleadingly at the doctor, dreading more medicine. The doctor fixed his assistant with a *certain* look.

Scarab was galvanised into action.

Hastily, a toffee was placed in Klumpet's hand.

ജ

A nightingale's sweet song soothed Mister Colic as he curled up on his bed. The gloopy-poop-poop had settled in a cold, uncomfortable glob in the pit of his stomach and he wasn't sure it was going to stay there for very long. He closed his eyes tight shut, listening to the undulating succession of rich notes, high then low, as they filtered through the air from the pine tree outside his home.

So, he didn't see a green, floppy hat bobbing its way past the window.

He didn't hear the front door opening ever so slowly and cautiously.

He didn't know *who* had placed the liquorice root and stomach-soothing tree bark juice next to his bed.

The soporific scent of jonquil floated up from a flower petal, placed gently on his pillow, and wafted the poorly man towards warm meadows and sunshine.

The door closed as quietly as it had been opened.

ℬ

Scarab consulted his list and put a big tick beside Mister Colic's name. The rain had begun once more; it was now not as heavy, but fell in a miserable drizzle making his hair curl slightly at the back of his neck. He pulled up the collar of his shiny, green coat and held the umbrella over Doctor Klumpet's glistening, bald head.

"A sore finger at Number 23," he stated. "I wonder whether it would be worth cutting off? Extra fees could be charged for the bandage use, you know."

The doctor considered this as they made their way down the street. Messy business, finger-cutting, he mused. He'd rather not, if it could be avoided. Still money was money and it was all in a good day's work.

A child answered the door at Number 23. She kept the chain on at first and peered warily from behind the crack.

"Hello?" she queried.

"Well hello ickle girlie! We're here to see your mumsie. Is she in?" Scarab spoke in syrupy tones, smiling his best sickly smile.

A shout was heard from inside the house.

"Is that the good doctor?"

"That it is, madam!" Scarab replied, importantly. "We believe you need expert assistance."

The girl was told to open the door properly and let the kind gentlemen in, which she duly did. She had a runny nose and her hair was in a tangle. Her face was tear-stained and she wore shabby clothes which no longer fitted her. Her laces were undone. A stench of over-cooked cabbage hung in the air. Scarab sniffed and pulled a face.

"Not much money to be made here, doctor," he whispered as they were shown through to the untidy living-room. "I shouldn't bother with the finger-cutting if I were you; we'd be chasing payment for months."

Doctor Klumpet nodded and inwardly gave a sigh of relief. Surgery was not his strength. He approached the woman whose face was flushed and had her finger in a bowl of icy water. She looked up at him, relief in her eyes.

"Oh Doctor Klumpet! Thank you so much for coming! It's my finger, you see. It's all swollen and sore."

So saying, she removed her hand from the bowl and held it out. There was a small cut on one side which had not healed properly. It looked angry and red and very, very painful.

The doctor considered it from a distance, rocking backwards and forwards on his heels as if in deep thought. Then he took a step nearer and gave the finger a sudden, sharp prod. The woman *shrieked* in agony and burst out crying. Her wailing set off their dog who had been minding his own business licking food from the dinner plates, and he howled in unison. Scarab leapt forward and, with a theatrical flourish, proffered a small tissue so she could mop her tears. Doctor Klumpet then accepted a rather large toffee and began to chew with vigour. The pair waited until she had settled down, her hand once more in the ice.

"Thank you for the tissue, Mister Scarab," the woman sobbed quietly. "You are so kind. Most thoughtful."

Scarab gave a courteous nod and began to unpack the medical supplies bag, as before. Klumpet regarded the clock on the wall, making a mental note of the passing minutes, and spoke for the first time since entering.

"Madam Septicus," he began, "it appears that your finger needs some attention."

"Oh yes, doctor! How clever you are! Indeed it does."

"Mister Scarab, please hand me the jar of leeches and a pair of the finest tweezers."

Scarab fumbled about in the bag and withdrew a pair of tweezers. They had a few of Klumpet's curly nostril hairs still stuck on them, but they wouldn't be noticed. The doctor unscrewed the lid of a jar and tweezered out a fine, brown leech. It was long and thin and in need of a good meal of blood. Once more, poor Madam Septicus offered her hand. The leech was dangled onto the sore finger, all watching whilst it latched on, to suck. The patient had become a peculiar shade of green and Scarab turned her face swiftly away so she couldn't see what was happening. The little girl watched in horrified silence from the doorway, her eyes growing ever wider.

Work done, the medical bag was packed up once more and Doctor Klumpet was ready.

57

"I'm in need of some fresh air," he called to Scarab over his shoulder as he prepared to leave the room. "Charge the patient the going rate, plus the price of one of the most exotic leeches, plus rental use of the finest tweezers money can buy." He shook out his umbrella ready to put up. A shower of rain droplets splattered Madam Septicus in the face. "And don't forget to add extra, to cover the cost of the tissue she had to use!"

Whilst the woman was comforting her daughter, ridding herself of the suction of the leech and reassuring the dog, she did not notice a green, floppy hat bobbing its way through the open window. She assumed, on returning to her seat, that the ice in her finger bath had melted and did not realise it had been replaced with slightly salty, cleansing fjord water. The honey-drenched bandage which was placed next to it must have been left by the kind Mister Scarab when she was looking for her purse. Oh how the dressing soothed her! She could feel her finger getting better already.

She couldn't quite explain the scattered petals on the floor though. She breathed in their scent and relaxed for the first time in days.

And so it was that the two Big Men were followed closely by a small tree-troll and a plain, brown nightingale. Each time a patient was visited and divested of his money by Klumpet and Scarab, an alternative medicine was either administered or left, along with flower petals, soaked in jonquil oil; calling cards, if you like. A cold poultice of dandelion leaves was pressed into position on a twisted ankle; an infusion of feverfew was given for a blinding headache; concoctions of berries and leaves from the depths of the forest were sipped to relieve sore throats, sneezes and rasping coughs. Each person fell into a deep slumber, breathing sweet scents and later awoke, feeling calm and refreshed. All began to recover in record time. All had a vague, dreamy notion of a green, floppy hat and the most beautiful birdsong they had ever heard, but none could quite explain them.

Finnr had watched and listened. He saw how the doctor mistreated his patients. He winced and grimaced at the cruelty, flinching at each stab of pain and careless treatment administered by the pair. His heart had thumped in excitement as he consulted his notebook, turning each page to find a cure. His fingers had trembled as he selected just the right tincture, mixed the best cordial and replaced his hat on his head. His troll-legs had shaken as he entered the houses of the Big People who needed his help, frightened that he would be found out, misunderstood and caught.

As Doctor Klumpet and Mister Scarab returned to their house, to count their ill-gotten gains and add up their profits, little did they realise that they had been followed all day. They didn't know that the doctor's bag had been spotted, and talk of patients on the tatty list had been overheard by a perching bird, tucked away in the undergrowth. Neither of them had any idea that their bad practice, their thieving, deceitful ways, had been witnessed by a medicine-maker who knew very much more than they did.

Luscinia flew ahead, returning to the forest and the comfort and safety of Finnr's nest-home. The cautious troll kept to the shadows until he was under cover of the trees. He padded along, sure-footed and quick, keeping as quiet as he could, thinking all the while about his potions and remedies.

At last he had been able to use his precious notebook!

At last he had been able to use his skills and test his knowledge!

It had been difficult to keep hidden – and tricky to gain access to the houses – but it *had* been possible and he *hadn't* been caught.

And it had been such fun!

He reached his rickety-pickety ladder, tired but happy, and began to climb upwards. He paused as he reached the rope bridge, to survey the forest and take a deep breath of the pine fragrance which surrounded him. Then Finnr the tree-troll, Finnr the medicine-maker, grinned cheerfully before bouncing and swinging his way to his beckoning feather bed.

Chapter Four

"Hmm... plots and plans. Plans and plots."

Everyone woke late the next morning.

Something wasn't quite right.

All was peculiarly silent, even though the sky had lightened and night had long since slipped away.

Slowly... slowly... one-by-one, the Big People in the town eventually rubbed their eyes, yawned and stretched. Sluggish hands fumbled for alarm clocks, to check – and then to shake! There was a sudden, startling *frenzy* and *outcry!* as curtains were flung open, the daylight making everyone blink, and small children were tumbled out of bed and bustled off to school.

The forest was a dim, green carpet of misty morning dampness, the only sound being the occasional drip of a water droplet from trees onto leaves on the woodland floor. No animals foraged in the ferns and bracken. No squirrels pinged twitchily from bouncy branch to bouncy branch. No insects rustled or scratched.

So quiet.

And all because Finnr had slept in.

Finnr had slept in for the first time ever; worn out.

The dawn chorus had not been conducted. It had not been whistled, chirruped, fluted, sung or indeed heard. The message had not been passed from tree to tree throughout the forest, from pine to birch to ash, from nature to trolls and Big People alike.

It was only when Luscinia took her drowsy head from beneath her wing that the tree-troll stirred. The nightingale's feathers fluffed briefly against his nose, rousing him at last. He snuffled under his soft blanket and pushed her gently to the floor in a dishevelled heap.

"Luscinia, im verisht shleepish dis morgy," Finnr murmured, trying to shake off his dreams. "Wass mattoori?"

The little bird tweeted melodically and pecked at Finnr's green, floppy hat. It fell off the twig hook and landed at a jaunty angle on the troll's head. He opened his eyes in surprise – and then he saw the daylight.

"Luscinia!" Finnr cried in sudden panic. "Dee morgy songli! Fastli, fastli!"

Gathering his dungarees in a scrunch and hopping to the rope bridge whilst still fastening his buttons, the sleepy troll hurried to waken the surrounding woodland. Loyal Luscinia followed with his weather-stick, ever ready to be at his side.

ॐ

As a result, Hildi and Thom had to eat a late breakfast that morning; Tailo and Scratchen, the mice, were grumbling and hungry; Grimo and Tracker were desperate to be let outside to do the things that cats and dogs have to do, and Thom had not yet set out in his boat. Grimhildr and Dotta had to scurry to tend to the animals in their care; the goats were blarting to be fed and milked. Only Hairy Bogley and Ulf welcomed the unusual quiet which surrounded them, as they snoozed away their night-time bogling activities, tucked up next to the fire they had lit in their home-cave.

However, when Finnr arrived, full of apologies and explanations, Hildi's little wooden table was laid at last for a fine meal and the water was just coming up to the boil. Pouring it onto nettle leaves in a rough clay pot, she smiled broadly at her tree-troll cousin, indicating he should take a seat.

"Mi, mi, Finnr," she chided gently. "U mekken oos laterig dis morgy. Vi u so shleepish? Dee tweetors shtay in nestlies en dee foresh animores nics varken oop todagen!"

Finnr grinned sheepishly as he accepted a hunk of bread and an oozing slice of melting cheese from Thom.

"Im badli troll todagen, mi dearigs," he admitted and proceeded to explain why he was so late up, telling them about his previous day. He told them how he and Luscinia had followed the Big Men as they visited each house; how they had listened at windows and doors; how they had crept inside, after the doctor and his lackey had left, in order to administer medicines and remedies. He told them what fun it had been and how satisfying it was to use his notebook properly at long last. Thom and Hildi listened in silence, a knot of concern growing in their stomachs. They understood Finnr's urge to practise his skills and they knew he had longed to put his potions of bark juice and leaf infusions to the test – but was this the right way? Whatever did Finnr think he was doing? Didn't he know how dangerous it was to have anything to do with the Big People?

"Es verisht dedden, Finnr," Thom commented at last, feeling it necessary to offer words of caution. "Dee Biggy Menor nics gooshty foor trolls."

"Yo, yo," Finnr nodded, understanding Thom's unease, but remaining confident. "Im verisht carefloosh en im creepori in dee homerigs liker littlelor morsi."

Thom and Hildi remained unconvinced. They were sure that Finnr *was* very careful – he was no fool – but he *could* have been seen. Worse still, he could have been caught! They knew too well how dreadful that would be, having rescued little Ulf from the clutches of the dreadful Birna and Ogmund a while ago.

There were very few trustworthy Big People.

Eventually, Luscinia's fluttering outside the window of the cosy home told Finnr it was time to leave. Thanking his cousins warmly and agreeing to take every care should he venture into the town once more, he pulled his hat floppily around his ears and hoppity-skipped down the path. Thom and Hildi waved as he took the turning to his tree house and, holding hands, they closed their wooden door quietly after him.

It was with great excitement and noise that Mister Scarab flung open Doctor Klumpet's door and ran inside. Scuttling up the stone steps, his breath catching in snatches, he grappled hastily with the door knob of the bedroom and burst in like an eager child on Christmas morning.

"Doctor! Doctor!" he cried. "Fame at last! We are the talky-talk of the town!"

Klumpet, like so many others that morning, had overslept but, unlike the others, on glancing at his bedside clock he had not rushed to embrace the day. His fat head was almost suffocated in the squash of his feather pillow, his piggy eyes were still tight shut and bubbly dribble ran down his chin. He made a sort of grunting noise but did not speak.

"Doctor, you must wake up!" Scarab continued, reaching into the enormous wardrobe for his employer's dressing gown. "Your medicines have actually worked!"

At this, Doctor Klumpet opened one eye. He scowled into his pillow, still not raising his head and slathered his spit back into his mouth.

"What do you mean, Scarab? What do you mean my 'medicines have *actually* worked'?"

"Just as I say, good Doctor! People have *actually* got better – and in record time too!"

Klumpet heaved himself up and sat in bed glaring at Mister Scarab in irritation. Such was the assistant's enthusiasm that he didn't notice the developing expression of thunder on the doctor's face, or that it was brewing into a storm.

"It's too good to be true," Scarab jabbered, breathlessly. "They're saying it's nothing short of a miracle! A mirrymiracle, I say! Perhaps we should re-brand ourselves as: 'The Miraculous Medicine Marvels!' No more: 'Plain, old Doctor K and the Amazing Mister Scarab', but: 'The Miraculous Medicine Marvels!' What do you think Doctor, hmm?"

Doctor Klumpet had heard quite enough. This blathering assistant was wearing him out and he hadn't even got out of bed yet.

"WHAT DO I THINK, MISTER SCARAB? WHAT DO I *THINK*?"

There was a sudden whimpering sound as Scarab ducked and covered his head with his hands as if expecting a smack. He cowered in front of the doctor, his knees beginning to shake. Klumpet lowered his tone and continued.

"I'll tell you what I think, Mister Scarab," he growled. "I think I take GREAT objection to your inference and I think you have got above yourself! Firstly, OF COURSE my medicines work! Secondly, OF COURSE people get better! And THIRDLY – perhaps *most importantly* – it is *I* who is amazing, not YOU!"

"Ah," agreed Scarab keeping his head bowed, not daring to look up. "Quite, quite so. Of course."

"My methods of leeching and choosing from the colour wheel aren't just a matter of luck, you know! I have been an illustrious doctor for many, many years," the doctor muttered, sounding a trifle hurt as he held out his sweaty pyjama arms to receive his robe. "I studied hard from all those: *'Teach Yourself to be a Doctor'* books, I picked up at the market. I even reached halfway through one of them!"

"Quite so, Doctor," Mister Scarab nodded, drawing the silk cord around his employer's protruding, blue-striped middle.

"...Scarab ducked and covered his head with his hands..."

He could sense the doctor was calming down slightly and he was anxious to keep it that way.

" '*Plain, old Doctor K'* indeed!" Klumpet snorted.

The dressing gown was fastened in silence and the fabric pulled and smoothed down at the front. It was only after offering a handful of calming, morning toffees, that Mister Scarab dared broach the subject again.

"If I may venture to say, Doctor," he began shakily, in breathy tones. "It just does seem a tinsy-winsy tad unusual, that's all."

The doctor was dreamily sucking through his teeth now. He wore a contented expression like a baby just given a dummy. His eyes were half-closed and his cheeks bulged. Suck, suck, suck.

"You *do* see don't you, Doctor? People are talking about being cured and, if we are totally honestly-honest with ourselves, we would have to admit this isn't what *usually* happens…" Mister Scarab's voice trailed off into uncertainty. He didn't want to put his case too strongly. The doctor cleared his throat from excess toffee goo and nodded ever so slightly. Scarab warmed to his theme.

"You see, if this really *is* the case we should make the most of it. *Capitalise* on it, if you get my meaning."

Klumpet looked a little baffled. In truth, he didn't understand what his employee was getting at. It all seemed a little too early in the morning for riddles and the effort of his earlier bawling had quite worn him out.

"What *exactly* do you mean, Mister Scarab?" he queried in a sticky sort of voice.

Scarab's face sharpened into a weasely, sneaky smile. "We should put our prices up, Doctor K!" he chuckled softly. "We can charge even *more* now!"

∞

What Mister Scarab had reported was indeed true. As he had made his way to the doctor's house, he had seen huddles of Big People talking and he had strained to overhear what he could. One or two of the men had even doffed their caps at him as he hurried past.

All most unusual.

The rapid improvement in health of the patients was still the talk of the town when Doctor Klumpet followed his assistant to attend more house calls, later that day. Mister Colic was standing upright and looking cheerful, no longer bent over double, in pain. Madam Septicus waved happily from the dirty window of her house as they passed, her finger bandaged, but obviously not sore anymore. Twisted ankles were strong again, headaches cleared and sore throats, sneezes and rasping coughs had been soothed. The doctor paraded himself down the street with a dignified air, waving a silk handkerchief at one and all, as if he were royalty.

"How good it feels to have the recognition I deserve, Mister Scarab," he boasted. "I am a true genius!"

"A genie-genius indeed, Doctor K," Scarab agreed.

"I am truly magnificent!"

"*Hugely* magnificent, Doctor K."

"A Doctor of all Doctors!"

Scarab was just about to reply once more, when Mister Colic came running over to them. He was waving a small bottle in one hand and in the other he appeared to have a small brown stick.

"This bark juice has worked a treat, Doctor Klumpet! I don't remember you leaving it – I must have been too ill at the time – but, believe me it's a wonder! And I have been chewing this liquorice root all morning. I feel a new man! Thank you good Doctor!"

Klumpet halted in his tracks.

Mister Scarab's eyes darted to the bottle and liquorice root being shown to them.

They both knew that *they* had not given Mister Colic these items.

Madam Septicus saw that the good doctor had stopped in the street. She rushed from the house and greeted him with an enormous hug, planting a kiss on his pink cheek.

"The dressing you left is so soothing, Doctor! My finger feels so much better. I really can't thank you enough. I saw that you had replaced my ice-water with some other, so I bathed it first then wrapped it up and within minutes, the throbbing had stopped."

Doctor Klumpet swallowed uncomfortably.

How very odd.

Mister Scarab though, seized the opportunity and spoke up. A small crowd had gathered and he knew this was a chance not to be missed.

"Well, well," he began. "Now you see for yourselves how wonderful the good Doctor Klumpet is! He can cure *any* ailment and is a most *stupendous* Practitioner of Medicine. You see before you, not just an ordinary – if rather overweight – gentleman, but an *expert* Medical Miracle-Maker!"

Klumpet smiled smugly at the throng (apart from a second or two when his face froze at the mention of his girth). This was perfect. Adoration from all! He had been waiting for this moment for a long time.

"Here you have," continued Scarab, thoroughly enjoying his own importance and gesturing between the two of them, "the Miraculous Medicine Marvels!" He paused for effect and then added: "At your service!" and bowing theatrically, he made a sweeping gesture with his hand.

The assembled crowd clapped appreciatively, including Doctor Klumpet who had got quite swept up in the whole thing. His face was getting pinker and pinker with excitement and a little speck of froth had appeared at the corner of his mouth. Mister Scarab nodded, assuming the expression of a very wise man and then, turning to the doctor, indicated that they should be on their way. Madam Septicus however, reached forward and tugged at Klumpet's sleeve. She looked conspiratorially around her before whispering, "And thank you for the flowers!" She blushed and batted her eyelids whilst tapping at her hair, feeling quite girly all of a sudden. Unfortunately, her secret whisper had not been very quiet and those closest heard her words. Doctor Klumpet was astonished and rather embarrassed.

Flowers?

What flowers?

Why would he waste precious money on flowers?

Before he could think of a response and before Mister Scarab could say something for him, there was a chorus of similar voices.

"Petals! Yes!"

"Flower petals! I had some too!"

"So sweet, they were! Like breathing in faerie dust!"

"Scattered on my pillow! I slept so soundly!"

Doctor Klumpet felt he was getting out of his depth. Something was happening in the town which he couldn't explain and although it cast him in a favourable light, it unnerved him too. It was when the talk then turned to dreams of a little man in a green, floppy hat that Mister Scarab decided enough was enough. Even *he* was losing the plot now. He grasped the doctor's arm firmly and began to escort him away.

"I thank you all most kindly," he called over his shoulder as they departed, "but we have other patients to see. The good Doctor's work is never done, you know!"

And so saying, the two hurried off down the street, leaving the Big People to compare their experiences.

ॐ

It did not take Mister Scarab long to work things out. He was lost in thought all the way back to Klumpet's house and there really was only one conclusion to be reached. The facts were that a) the Big People had recovered from a variety of illnesses and conditions, b) realistically this had little to do with Doctor Klumpet's expertise – because he had none – and c) natural remedies and flower petals had been left at the scene. He also remembered with a sickly lurch of his stomach, that there were reports of a little man in a green, floppy hat…

A little man.

A green, floppy hat.

Woodland herbs and remedies.

Drat! No doubt about it – a *troll* was out and about!

That night, as Scarab lay in bed, he clenched his fists and ground his teeth. He fidgeted and twitched even more than usual. This could spell disaster for them. If the Big People also worked out what was going on, he and Doctor Klumpet could be out of a job! That would never do! Where would his dreams of riches and wealth be then? What would happen to his vision of a massive mansion and luxurious yacht? All it would take would be for the people of the town to get together and talk amongst themselves.

He had to think of a plan. A scheme. A plot.

In the darkness, a crafty smile lit Mister Scarab's face. His toes wiggled in excitement. Suddenly, he sat upright.

If they were cunning enough, this situation could play very nicely into their hands, actually. Very nicely indeed. He and Doctor Klumpet had to make this work in *their* favour. All they had to do was to get the troll to do their work for them.

All they had to do was… *to get the troll!*

Chapter Five

"Set a trap. A trap is set."

Finnr whistled cheerily as he packed his hat and gathered his notebook, the next day. He felt happy and carefree after having had a good rest, and now refreshed, he was keen to venture out once more. The birds in his nest-home heard his tunes and joined in with their own music. The turtle doves turr-turred, the wood larks titloo-titlooed and the tree pipits soared into the sky singing, "tsip-tsip-tsip, chup-chup-chup," before spiralling back down, relishing the rush of air under their wings. Luscinia saved her song for the end of the day when the others would be tucking their heads quietly into their feathers. She loved to warble at the moon, as the stars twinkled and winked. When all was quiet, she would send her sweet melody out into the darkness of the forest, each note harmonising with the next in a lilting lullaby.

Now though, there was work to be done.

Luscinia flew hither and thither, fetching and carrying for Finnr. Flower petals were collected, bark and berry juices were selected and final touches to medicines were perfected, until at last the tree-troll sprang onto his rope bridge, his hairy feet making it sway and creak.

"Comli Luscinia!" he cried, looking back to his tree house. "Ve goingor helpen dee Biggy Menor wit dee problemoris. Ve mekken monkee-monkee wit dee biggy, fatli Klumpi-Pumpet en ve hab gooshty fonnerig, yo?"

The devoted little nightingale trilled her reply and flew to land lightly on Finnr's shoulder. He chuffed her fondly. Seconds later, they had descended the rickety-pickety ladder, rung-by-rung, and were making their way to the town.

ℰ

As always the two companions, troll and bird, were careful to keep to the shadows and secrecy of the bushes, peeking out to check the way forward was clear, before moving on. Luscinia flew ahead a little, her bright eyes alert, her whistling chirrups sending warnings when necessary. Finnr followed, green, floppy hat pulled down so low that the brim almost rested on his long nose. With weather-stick in hand, he made quick but cautious progress, ever wary of potential danger. He understood this new game of his was risky – and he certainly didn't intend to let his guard drop – but the thrill of using his precious notebook and carefully concocted medicines was now irresistible.

The streets were a flurry of activity, as Big People went about their daily business. Shop doorbells rang and clanged as men and women entered to buy all manner of things from cuttlefish to cabbages, from hairnets to hammers, from trampolines to trumpets. Deliveries were made out of the backs of vans, boxes being stacked next to ever-increasing piles of rubbish at the side of the road. Chatterers chatted, gossips gossiped, hands were shaken and cheeks were kissed in greetings and farewells. Children ran and chased each other noisily in the school playground until a shrill whistle sounded and they disappeared inside, to be consumed once more by number and word monsters. Nobody noticed a little troll scurrying between side-streets and hiding behind litter bins. Nobody noticed an ordinary-looking, plain, brown bird which dipped and dived, fluttered and flew. Everyone was too busy with the hustle and bustle of everyday living.

A little way off, a familiar figure bumbled along. His loud, checked trousers, still caked with mud from the puddles of previous days, flapped about his ankles as he made his way down the main street. From time to time, he stopped to fumble around in his old, battered medical bag, to retrieve a toffee which he stuffed into his mouth, bending over so all could see the roundness of his great bottom. He discarded the wrapper thoughtlessly onto the road. Finnr watched his progress with interest.

"Urnli Klumpi-Pumpet todagen, Luscinia," he commented quietly, wondering why the doctor was on his own. "Wass mattoori wit dee udder biggy oon? Dee creepori beetloosh, Scarab?"

Finnr's little friend didn't answer. She cocked her head to one side in an enquiring sort of way and continued to watch the Big Man.

Doctor Klumpet cleared his throat. The trouble with toffees, he noted to himself, was that they did get rather gooey

"She cocked her head to one side in an enquiring sort of way…"

in his mouth and could, on occasion, stick his tonsils together a bit. He swallowed a gobbet of sugary syrup and ran his tongue over his teeth. Glutinous strings, like over-stretched elastic bands, needed sucking before he could speak clearly. And today he needed to speak clearly. It was of vital importance that his words should be heard. And, hopefully, *overheard* by a certain someone...

Looking around him, with a puzzled expression in his piggy eyes, the doctor said out loud: "Tut, tut! Today of all days, when I'm so very, very busy!"

He paused.

From a distance, Finnr watched and listened.

"Just when I need him most, he goes and takes the day off. Just can't get the staff nowadays!"

Klumpet consulted a tatty piece of paper.

Finnr watched and listened.

"Now what *was* the number of that house?" questioned the doctor, turning the paper over and upside down as if he had trouble reading the writing on it. "Ah yes! Not far actually, but I must hurry if I'm to get there on time!"

The scruffy note fluttered down from his fingers and landed in the street. Luscinia flew from Finnr's shoulders and, as Klumpet proceeded on his way, she pecked at it to pick it up and deliver it so the medicine-troll could take a look. Like the Big Man had done, Finnr turned it over in his hairy hands. The writing on the note seemed to make no sense at all. It looked just like a scribble to him. There seemed to be neither a number of a house, nor any definable words written down. Why should the doctor pretend to consult a note with nothing of any sense written on it? Finnr took off his hat, carefully keeping his medicines and remedies in place, and scratched his head.

How very strange!

Here was the peculiar Doctor Klumpi-Pumpet, without the assistance of his faithful Mister Scarab, trying to find a patient's house by considering a chewed up piece of paper, with no real writing on it. Whatever could this mean? What *was* going on today? Finnr replaced his hat and, munching a few chamomile flowers he found in his pocket, followed thoughtfully. Without doubt, the doctor was about to visit a patient. He had said so out loud, hadn't he? And without doubt, he had his bag of medical supplies with him, didn't he? Maybe the note was written in special doctors' sort of writing so other people couldn't understand it – patient confidentiality or something. Whatever the situation, thought Finnr, he would still follow at a distance, but be extra careful until he was more certain.

બ

After a short time, the Big Man stopped walking and once more addressed the air around him, talking to nobody in particular.

"Here we are then! This is the house. Haven't been *here* before. No, never!" Klumpet paused. "I say: I haven't been *here* before! What a pity Mister Scarab can't assist me today.

79

He must be having a wonderful time *visiting his relations*. Good job he packed my medical bag before he left!"

Finnr listened to this, baffled. Why was the doctor talking to himself? Why did he keep emphasising that Mister Scarab was away for the day? Presumably this was the house of another patient, the one on his scribbled note, but in that case, why was the doctor letting himself in, instead of knocking at the door? Finnr hadn't seen where the key had come from as the bush he was hiding in obscured his view a little, but he definitely heard the turn of a key in the lock.

The weather-stick twitched as a cloud suddenly blotted out the sun and the sky darkened unexpectedly. A chilly breeze rustled the leaves and lifted the brim of Finnr's hat slightly. Luscinia's feathers ruffled and she peeped a note of warning.

Something wasn't quite right today.

As the door closed behind Klumpet, all the troll could hear was the beating of his own heart as it thumped in his little, hairy chest. He waited, keeping absolutely stock-still and silent, holding his breath so he could listen. After a minute or so, there was the sound of a window being opened. It smacked back against the outside wall and a dirty curtain flapped over it. Voices could be heard from inside.

"So, Missus – erm – "

"Hood-winker. Missus Hood-winker," sniggered the reply.

"Quite. You seem to be rather poorly, Missus – erm – Hood-winker."

Finnr strained to catch every word. Slowly, he crept out from his bush and positioned himself below the open window,

80

making sure he kept his head low to avoid the tip of his hat showing. He held his weather-stick tightly in case he needed it to defend himself and he gripped his notebook under his arm, lest he should drop it with a sudden thud.

"Yes, Doctor Klumpy-Klumpet," came the thin, reedy voice. "I'm very poorly-oorly. I have these big spots, see?"

There was a brief moment of silence.

"And this rainbow rashy-rash here, see?"

Another pause.

"And my totie-toes are rather green!"

Finnr frowned slightly. What an odd set of symptoms! He would have to see these for himself if he were going to be able to administer the right medicine. He would have to look in his notebook very carefully, perhaps way-back to his notes from ancient troll times. Maybe he would have to combine more than one remedy for this unfortunate person! His weather-stick pulled in his grip slightly. It seemed to be trying to get Finnr to move away from the window and leave this house. The tree-troll yanked hard on it and it became still once more. Luscinia, from a safer distance, warbled a quick message, but Finnr merely put a finger to his lips to indicate she should keep quiet. This was too fascinating to miss! A new set of symptoms to work with! A new remedy to be concocted, on the spot!

After a short while, a small piece of paper rustled and there was a sucking, slurping sound. Doctor Klumpet cleared his throat of a sticky sort of clog and announced that he was on his way.

"I'll leave you with this medicine then, Missus Hood-winker. Make sure you take it three times a day and bathe your

81

toes in frog spawn. Squidge it through thoroughly, mind, or it won't work." Then he added, rather more loudly: "I'll leave this window open for you, so you can get some fresh air!"

In a sudden rush, Finnr scurried back to his bush as the door was flung open and Klumpet strode down the path, humming loudly, his watery eyes creased in a satisfied sort of smile. Funny. There had been no mention of a fee this time. There had been no hurrying to find a purse or a wallet with which to pay. There had been no pleading of poverty and for extra time.

The doctor's heavy footsteps faded surprisingly suddenly, too. One second there they were *pounding* down the path, and the next they had vanished into thin air. It was as if he had lost his heavy shoes and was in just his socks all of a sudden, tiptoeing like a thief! Was that possible? Would he do that? Finnr shook his head. Ridiculous notion! It *was* true that at the same time as Klumpet's footsteps disappeared, Luscinia sent a sudden, agitated series of danger-tweets, but the troll was far too intrigued by the situation to pay any attention and shushed her with an impatient wave of his hand. The Big Man must have taken a turn down the road and the houses had swallowed up his footfalls. That was all. No matter, Finnr decided, he was sure the Big Man had gone and now was the time to act. What could go wrong? He had his bottle of jonquil oil so he knew the patient would sleep well after his visit and remember him only as a dream. He had his notebook and his trusty hat of tinctures and potions – and he was sure he could find a cure.

Leaning his weather-stick up against the wall and tucking his notebook securely into his dungarees, the agile troll grasped the window ledge and hooked one hairy foot over. In a trice, he was in the room where only minutes before, the Big Doctor had been standing.

The little brown nightingale whistled sorrowfully from her branch. Her call went unheeded.

It took a few seconds for Finnr's eyes to adapt to the gloom of the room. Although the sky outside had darkened slightly, it was still lighter than inside this house. All was neat and tidy; the only things out of place were a few toffee papers on the floor and a bottle green overcoat, which was slung on the table. A scrawny figure was sitting upright in an armchair, with legs resting on a footstool. A lanky strand of hair fell across her closed eyes.

She seemed to be asleep.

Finnr approached, cautiously. He peered at the Big Person's face and tried to make out the features. A yellow headscarf was wrapped tightly around her head like a bandana, covering the rest of her hair.

She appeared to have stubble on her chin!

A strange, breathy rasping sound issued from pursed lips; it was not quite a snore, nor was it normal breathing. The mouth was weasely and curled up at one corner slightly, in a knowing sort of smirk. A raggedy shawl was wrapped around her shoulders and she wore slippers on her feet.

And my goodness what big feet she had!

They stuck out at the end of bare, hairy legs, rather like paddles. Finnr looked at the blanket which covered her. It was being gripped tightly, the knuckles of both hands showing white. How could anyone clutch a blanket so firmly when they were asleep?

And my goodness what big, bony fingers she had!

They looked strong, as if they could squeeze hard. They looked grasping and grabbing. Every now and then they fidgeted. Maybe Missus Hood-winker was dreaming?

Finnr began to feel uncomfortable. He was sure the patient *had* called herself *Missus* Hood-winker, but she was a very strange sort of woman. He looked for signs of spots but there were none to be seen. Quickly, he searched her skin for evidence of a rainbow-coloured rash, but apart from broken veins, black leg hairs and other unsightly blemishes, the skin showed nothing unusual.

Finnr thought back to what else he had overheard. What *was* the other symptom? Ah yes! Green toes! He pulled out his notebook and began to flick through the pages searching for information about spots, rashes and green toes. He shook his head as he scanned page after page of carefully logged medical matters. Nothing! Perhaps there was another symptom. Perhaps he should remove a slipper from one of those huge feet and take a look for himself…

Quietly. Quietly.

Slowly. Slowly.

Carefully.

SO carefully.

A tug here. A wiggle there.

Pull – pull – pull –

"Gotcha!!"

In a heart-stopping second, Hood-winker lunged forwards from the chair and made a sudden ***grab!***

The bony fingers gripped hard and pinched Finnr's flesh. A grinning face with two sharp, clever eyes was thrust, piercingly close and the terrified troll could feel the Big Person's breath on him. As Finnr struggled to free himself, Missus Hood-winker's headscarf was pulled off, revealing a *man's* greasy hair and face!

"DOCTOR! DOCTOR! I'VE GOT 'IM!"

There was a thundering noise of heavy feet as Doctor Klumpet burst through the door to join them.

"HELP ME HOLD HIM, DOCTOR! HE'S A WRIGGLY LITTLE WORMY-WORM!"

"COMING SCARAB, COMING! HOLD HIM TIGHT!"

The doctor blundered his way towards Mister Scarab, red in the face, hands outstretched and with spit flying from his mouth. Finnr kicked and fought, twisting and writhing in Scarab's grip. His green, floppy hat fell off and the contents clattered to the floor, broken and spilled. The sweet scent of jonquil filled the air. Klumpet's right foot stepped into the spreading pool of oil and he skidded as if on ice, legs stretching apart in different directions and arms flailing. He grappled wildly at the air to regain his balance, but only succeeded in grabbing Mister Scarab. Clumsily, the doctor slid further on the oil, his feet trying but failing to get a grip, and he ended up face-down on the footstool. In the kerfuffle,

Scarab fell off his armchair onto the floor, squealing and squawking, releasing his hold on the troll.

"GRAB HIM, YOU FOOL!" bellowed Klumpet, turning his sweating face out of the footstool cushion to draw breath. "DON'T LET HIM ESCAPE!"

The doctor's assistant struggled to his feet and dived at Finnr, but the little troll was too quick. He swept up his hat from the floor, just as Luscinia arrived at the open window with his weather-stick.

"Gooshty tweetor, Luscinia!" panted Finnr. "Im comli fastli, fastli!"

He took the weather-stick from the little bird and held it out towards the advancing form of Scarab, who was crawling through broken bottles of berry juices and leaf infusions.

"Shtop en shtay, Mister Beetloosh!" commanded Finnr in a threatening fashion. "U badli en im goingor strikor u!"

Mister Scarab whined slightly and covered his head with his bony hands, cringing like a dog afraid of its master. Finnr took his chance. He leapt out of the window and ran. He ran as fast as his little troll-legs would carry him, teeth chattering like a monkey, lungs on fire, back through the streets of the town, towards the forest.

80

As Doctor Klumpet rubbed his fat knees and sore legs, Mister Scarab cleared up the mess. Presently, he sat back on his heels and began to grin. Then to chortle. Then to LAUGH OUT LOUD! The doctor looked at him, quizzically.

"The silly-billy puny troll has left something behind, Doctor K!" announced Scarab, his voice filled with glee. "Look what I've found, knockety-knocked under the chair!"

Klumpet stretched out his hand to his assistant.

He was passed a notebook.

A simple, leather-bound notebook.

"A simple, leather-bound notebook."

Chapter Six

"Regrets and repercussions."

At the break of dawn, having woken the birds in haste, Finnr scrambled along his rope bridge and down the rickety-pickety ladder to the forest floor. His mind was in a whirl. He had spent a dreadful night, sleepless and agitated. His little, hairy legs were sore from running so fast the day before, and his arms were bruised from when Scarab had tried to detain him. His gentle troll-heart still jumped and bumped as he re-lived the fright he had when pounced upon, and he trembled as he recalled the panic of his escape.

Why hadn't he listened to Luscinia's warning calls?

Why hadn't he taken heed of his weather-stick as it tried to pull him away from the house?

The house. Finnr groaned inwardly. He should have realised it was Doctor Klumpet's house. He should have thought more carefully about how the doctor was behaving. There had been nothing written on his tatty piece of paper and yet still Klumpet knew where to go. He even entered the house with a key and didn't have to knock! He didn't ask for payment. And when those footsteps went so quiet, so quickly, why didn't Finnr work out that the doctor was sneaking round the back? Then of course there were the symptoms – so peculiar! And her name – what was it again? Missus Hood-winker. *Missus Hood-winker!* Oh dear. The sad troll shook his head at his own stupidity and pride. He had been so wrapped up in his excitement at using his notebook and finding a new remedy that he had forgotten to be cautious. He wanted to be so clever and proud of himself that he overlooked the clues which had been staring him in the face. Even the weather had changed and he had ignored the sign.

What was he going to do now?

His precious notebook was in the hands of the Big People. It was in Doctor Klumpet's possession.

All those irreplaceable notes of medicines and remedies, recorded faithfully day after day, week after week, year after year: a lifetime's work in charcoal scribbling and feather quill writing. All those samples of roots, bark, seeds and leaves. All those ancient cures passed down from generations before him. Lost.

Gone.

Finnr dashed hot tears away from his old eyes as he stumbled through the trees, his troll-tail drooping. How could he have been so stupid? He could not clear his head of his distress. The only thing he could think of doing, was to go to Hildi and Thom. He needed their comfort and advice. Trolls always turned to each other in times of trouble; their families extended through all the forests and mountains, over the deep fjords and beyond. It was a network of support and love which did not chastise or finger-wag. Every troll knew they could rely wholeheartedly on others for help when it was needed.

And Finnr certainly did need help that morning. Help – and a soothing cup of nettle tea.

∞

The moment that Mister Scarab had passed the notebook into Doctor Klumpet's hands, a shout of triumph had filled the air.

"WHO NEEDS THE TROLL?" Klumpet had yelled, with a great, deep belly laugh. "WE HAVE HIS SECRETS!"

"Indeedy-deedy, Doctor K," Scarab replied with a self-satisfied smile. "To catch and keep the nuisance-troll would have been a tricky-icky problem and this way we can still use his knowledge. Everyone will think we are quite brilliant!"

"Which we *are*, of course, Scarab – well, *I* am at least!"

Mister Scarab chose to ignore this jibe and continued.

"All we need to do is to read the troll's notes and go out there, mending people and making lots of divine dosh, lovely lolly, cool cash! No more complaints about us, just compliments and thanks. Just think how loved we – *you* – will be!"

The doctor closed his eyes and imagined for a second how wonderful it would be to feel so well-respected. Loved, even. He wasn't sure he had *ever* been loved.

Mister Scarab closed his eyes and imagined how wonderful it would be to get their hands on even more money. Visions of sports cars, mansions and private yachts filled his head once more. He tried to calculate how much longer they would have to work until they had got enough money to live this life of luxury. He thought of what they charged every five minutes; perhaps they could put it up again? He tried to multiply in his head how many patients they would have to cure, and at what cost, but he got tangled up in mental mathematical knots and had to give up. One thing was certain, however long it took, this notebook would make a huge difference to them and their money-making abilities! What a stroke of luck!

The doctor did not retire to his bed that evening. Instead, he drew up his old, leather chair and opened Finnr's notebook. He instructed Scarab to pass him his reading glasses, open a bag of his favourite toffees and make up a flask of hot chocolate to see him through the night. When his assistant closed the door and left, Klumpet was hunched over the ivory parchment pages, toffee drool coating his pink lower lip like an oil slick.

Page after page was turned with one licked finger.

Lick. Lick. Lick.

Time ticked by slowly.

Tick. Tick. Tick.

After a couple of hours of sitting alone and in silence, Doctor Klumpet yawned and sat back in his chair. It creaked as he did so, his weight being rather too much for its worn wooden frame. He removed his glasses and rubbed his eyes, making them even redder and more swollen. This task was not as easy as it seemed. He poured himself the dregs of his chocolate and swallowed them in one greedy gulp. He wiped his mouth on the back of one hand and, with sticky fingers, picked up the notebook once more. Reading and understanding all this was quite hard work, much harder than Klumpet expected. Not only was the writing in an unfamiliar troll-style, but also there were little codes and marks in the margins which indicated quantities, he presumed, but made no sense to him. Whilst some parts of the book were sketchy, charcoal notes, other parts were written in a flowery, difficult hand and at such length that the doctor found his head nodding and his eyes closing. However, the trickiness of the reading was not the main problem. With patience, time, his brilliant brain and Mister Scarab's assistance, they were certain to be able to make sense of it. No, the main problem with Finnr's notes was more difficult to resolve.

The ingredients.

The ingredients were unfamiliar to Doctor Klumpet. He had used leeches and his gloopy-poop-poop for as long as he could remember. His Wonderful Wheel of Medicine Magnificus had served him well in giving him a grave air of mystery, if not magician's ability. His patients always paid him so they *must* be satisfied! And yet, in his heart, he knew their recovery was more to do with good luck than anything he prescribed. So this lengthy book of troll notes, with its use of balsam, fenugreek, liquorice, wild garlic, hibiscus and something called jonquil oil, was all very unfamiliar to him. What were all these strange leaves and powders? Where did you find these lotions and tinctures? How did you bottle infusions and bark juices?

Doctor Klumpet sighed and shook his head. This was not going to be easy.

Not easy at all.

Thom reached into the dresser and pulled out a small, green bottle of Troll-Cherry Wine, kept for exactly such emergencies as this. He poured a small amount into a rough, clay mug and passed it solemnly to Finnr. The tree-troll's hands shook as he took it.

"Thanken, thanken Thom," he whispered hoarsely.

Hildi settled herself next to him at the table and patted his arm comfortingly. This was all very upsetting. Both she and Thom knew how much Finnr's notebook meant to him, and how important it was that this knowledge be kept safe. They had doubted the wisdom of going into the town to try out medicines on the Big People and had urged caution, but who were they to tell Finnr what he should and shouldn't do?

"Shhh, mi dearig," Hildi murmured softly. "U es verisht sadli. Sitli en shtay en feelen happli soonig."

The notebook was lost, but at least Finnr was safe.

ℰ

Days passed. Sunshine and clouds swapped places in the sky. Rain pattered onto the trees. The forest was hushed and dark at night. It was gloomy and dull throughout the day. The birds' songs were not so bright and cheerful; the woodland animals went about their business silently. The rickety-pickety ladder did not creak. The rope bridge did not sway and swing.

94

Finnr sat with knees drawn up to his chest, sulking.

Luscinia, faithful as ever, kept him company. She knew when to stay quiet and she knew when to whistle a gentle, pretty song to bring a slight smile to his old, whiskery face. She encouraged him to eat at the right times and kept him warm by nestling under his chin at night.

In the town, however, all was not so quiet. As time went by, the Big People became frustrated. It had become difficult to contact Doctor Klumpet; he never answered his door or his telephone. Mister Scarab always declared he was too busy to listen when he hurried past, on his way to work. The pair seemed preoccupied with some project or other and had no time for people's illnesses at the moment.

It wasn't that Doctor Klumpet had forgotten the people he needed to look after. It wasn't that Mister Scarab wanted to waste time, not making money. It was just that they were engrossed in Finnr's notebook. As Klumpet struggled to read the words, Scarab made a long list of ingredients. He tried to group them under different headings for different illnesses, desperate to make some sense of the troll's work. Pieces of paper were strewn over the floor of the doctor's living room, along with toffee wrappings and discarded mugs, stained with tea, coffee and chocolate. The two of them were sure that it would be worth it in the end. Once they had the medicine-troll's secrets, they could go out into the town and become rich and famous!

"Finnr sat with knees drawn up to his chest, sulking."

After a while, a hand-written notice appeared on the doctor's front door. It read:

DO NOT RING OR KNOCK!

The esteemed Doctor Klumpet and his most valued assistant, Mister Scarab, are extremely busy learning new skills and lots of clever stuff you could not possibly understand. They cannot, at present, deal with any of your bugs, germs or injuries. Please put off being ill until next week.

Always at your service ~

With thanks and felicitations to you all.

The Big People snorted when they read this and word passed around that the doctor was not prepared to help them. Just as the note said, they *didn't* understand what the new skills or clever stuff could be. What they *did* understand was that some of them were poorly, including a few children, and they needed advice.

"'Always at your service,' he says! Pah!" spat one woman, indignantly. "He's hardly 'at our service' if he won't even answer his door!"

"And he calls himself a doctor!" retorted another. "He's a disgrace, that's what he is! How can we 'put off being ill'?"

"It's a funny business, no mistake," commented a third. "There's something going on in there that he doesn't want us to know about. What do you think they're both up to?"

And so the gossip continued, from shop doorway to shop doorway, from school gate to home letterbox, up the streets and down. Small niggles grew into grumbles and the grumbles grew into growls. A couple soon became a group and the group soon became a crowd. Eventually, when no one could talk of anything else, a meeting was called at the little chapel which stood on top of the hill at the far end of town.

Something had to be done.

၆၁

Finnr raised his head from his knees and put a hand to one ear, listening.

"Wass dee soundor, Luscinia?" he asked his little bird friend as she cocked her head enquiringly. "Im thinken dingle-donglor es in foresh. Vi?"

The two stayed still and listened intently. Presently the ringing bell sounded again.

"Yo, yo," nodded Finnr, getting to his feet and hitching up his dungarees. "Es dingle-donglor. In foresh. Verisht strangeror! Ve hab nay dingle-donglors in foresh – urnli tweetors en udder animores. Vi dingle-donglor mekken soundor?"

Curiosity aroused, Finnr scampered along his rope bridge for the first time in days. He scrambled down the rickety-pickety ladder, jumping the last two rungs, and set off to investigate. He was tired of feeling sorry for himself. It was boring being unhappy. It was about time he had something to do again. If he had no notebook to write in and no Big People to practise on, he would have to find out why there was a bell ringing in the forest. That would pass the time nicely until lunch.

As he got closer, his troll-steps slowed. Luscinia flew on ahead to check the path was safe and Finnr kept to the shelter of the trees. Suddenly, the nightingale issued a quick peep of warning so he ducked down, taking full notice of her this time. His hairy knees began to tremble and the troll-fur prickled on the back of his neck. Excitement was one thing; taking risks was quite another. He did not intend to get into trouble again. The bell rang a couple more times and then fell silent. Footsteps were heard disappearing through the forest and at last, Finnr decided it was time to take a look.

A woman was walking away from the trees, towards the town. She was neither hurrying nor dawdling, just walking as if it were perfectly normal to come into the forest, ring a loud hand bell and then leave. Behind her, and in front of Finnr, was a wooden crate upon which the bell had been left. There seemed to be nothing in the crate. It merely served as a makeshift table. Luscinia tooted a signal of safety and the troll approached, cautiously.

Underneath the bell was a piece of paper. There was neat writing on it. Without letting the clapper either ding or dong, Finnr pulled the paper out and considered it carefully. He looked around him to see if there was anyone else nearby who might be expecting a letter, left on a wooden crate, in the middle of the forest, underneath a bell.

He was quite alone.

"Luscinia," the tree-troll called softly. "Luscinia, comli heer en helpen meer. Biggy Menor leftig notoori!"

Sitting comfortably on a mossy stump at the base of a tall pine, Finnr began to read. His lips moved quietly as his finger followed the lines on the paper. Then he began a slow smile.

It seemed that the Big People had a Big Problem. Their doctor, a certain Doctor Klumpet, was not attending to their needs right now. Some of them required medicine or advice and did not know where to turn. A little while ago, a few members of the town had visits from Klumpet and his assistant, Mister Scarab, but something rather unusual had happened. Each person had slipped into a deep, blissful sleep. Each person had found flower petals scattered on the floor or their pillow and each had a vague notion of a small, hairy man in a green, floppy hat having been there.

Finnr grinned widely at this.

"Es meer, Luscinia! Es secresht Finnr in Biggy Menor homerigs!"

In addition to these common experiences, all had medicines or aid left, that they didn't remember Doctor Klumpet talking about. Stranger still, these remedies worked like magic! After much conversation the Big People had decided, ridiculous as it seemed, that a troll must be involved and they were now trying to contact him, for help.

"Es meer, Luscinia!" Finnr exclaimed again. "Im helpen dee Biggy Menor. Im happli, happli troll!"

He was delighted to read that his medicines had been a success. He had wanted to test his knowledge and the remedies in his notebook for so long – and now he knew they worked! He jumped to his feet and ran round and round the base of the tree until he was quite giddy, waving the note and hooting: "Doctoori Finnr! Doctoori Finnr!" He swayed a little when he finally stopped dashing round in circles and noticed that on the back of the note was more writing. There were details of illnesses and requests for medicines to be left.

So this was how it was going to work.

Finnr laughed with relief. He could collect notes from the Big People, when they rang the bell in the forest. He would work out which remedies to gather from his tree house and leave them back at the crate. No more risky visits into homes in the town. No more scary following of Doctor Klumpet and

Mister Scarab. It would keep him busy and test his skills. Perfect.

Then Finnr frowned a little.

As long as he could remember what he had written in his notebook…

Chapter Seven

"A bird in the hand..."

It was Pipi and Fug, the two flaggermusses, who told the other forest trolls what Finnr was up to. Living as rescue bats with Dotta and Grimhildr, they thought nothing of flitting their way through the trees to investigate the ringing of a bell which sounded each morning. Nocturnal habits were not for them; they were happy to find out woodland news at any time of the day or night. Having been dispatched to find the source of the dinging and the donging, they had quickly found the crate and the hand bell. They had hung upside down from a branch nearby, watching and listening keenly, and when the Big Person left, they found out to their surprise that it didn't take long for Finnr to arrive. It was obvious that he approached warily, before collecting a piece of paper and disappearing through the trees, dancing and laughing. The two little flaggermusses waited, swing-swanging and humming batty tunes, and soon they saw the tree-troll return with bottles and jars holding powders and syrups. Within the hour, Dotta and Grimhildr knew all about it and had hurried to their sister's little home, a short distance away. Hildi and Thom, welcoming as always, quickly offered seats at the wooden table, poured nettle tea to sip and handed out warm bilberry tarts to munch.

All of them had heard the bell ringing, just once a day, a few hours after sunrise, but before noon. It had made a strange sound in the forest and both trolls and animals had been alarmed at first. When the ding-donging was repeated, day after day, their curiosity took over and it was then that they had decided to send Pipi and Fug to investigate. From what they learned, it was clear a regular routine had been established. It was clear Finnr was giving medicines to the Big People, by arrangement. It was clear he was perfectly happy about it.

The trolls talked at length about the situation. They knew how hard Finnr had worked to compile his precious notebook and how desperately upset he had been when he had left it behind, in the Big Man's house. Although it would be very much more difficult for him, they knew he would want to continue to make medicines as best he could, and they all agreed he must be enjoying his new work. No doubt Finnr would have to cast his mind back to all he had written before, and unfortunately much information was now lost in the mists of time, but they knew he would be determined to carry on. Eventually, the gathering of trolls decided it could do no harm as long as the Big People did not come close to their own dwellings. In fact, they reasoned, this was a far safer way for Finnr to carry out his work than before. The greater the distance he could keep from the Big People, the better.

"Finnr es carefloosh im thinken," concluded Thom. "Dee Biggy Menor needen helpen en Finnr es happli troll."

"Yo, yo," agreed the others, nodding sagely. "Nay problemori wit Finnr!"

"Gooshty nettli tay, Hildi," smiled Dotta holding out her cup for a refill.

§

With a sigh of relief, Doctor Klumpet closed Finnr's notebook and pushed it to the far side of his desk. Mister Scarab dotted the last "i" and crossed the last "t" on his list of ingredients and clipped his pen neatly into his top pocket.

"Well Scarab, what do you think? Do you think we have listed everything? Do you think we know what the little, hairy troll uses?" The doctor paused. "Do you think there are any more toffees in the cupboard?"

Scarab considered these questions whilst rubbing a weary hand over his tired eyes. Actually, he didn't really know *what* to think. Surely they had listed everything by now! They had worked for days and days, and nights and nights, peering at the strange writing and deciphering each word. Without doubt, they knew *what* the troll used, but quite *where* to get these things from was another matter entirely. He opened the doctor's cupboard and searched for more toffees. There was a paper bag full of them, stashed at the back. They were probably a bit old by now as they had been bought a while ago to be kept as emergency rations, but they were the only ones available because neither he, nor the doctor, had been out of the house for such a long time. He handed them to Klumpet.

"These are the only toffee-toffees in the cupboard, Doctor K," he apologised. "I will go out directly and buy some more."

The doctor waved him off impatiently and within minutes, Scarab was outside breathing fresh air for the first time in a week. He was keen to leave the stale smell of the room in which they had been working and certainly he needed time to clear his head and think. In truth, he was rather concerned. He could see only problems lying ahead. Now the doctor had the troll's notebook, he would want to use it. This Scarab agreed with; it was the perfect way to make more money and as such was invaluable information. However, he could use it only if he had the *ingredients*. The ingredients were not to be found in any of the shops in *this* town – or in any *other* town for that matter. They were not the usual sort of medical supplies at all. The assistant frowned to himself as he set off down the road. Would this put Doctor Klumpet off? He frowned even more.

No.

It would not. He knew the doctor would demand the ingredients were found and brought to him, ready to pack into his medical bag. It would be Scarab's responsibility to locate them. Sighing wearily, he turned a corner in the road and saw the toffee shop ahead. There *had* to be a way of getting hold of the powders and juices and concentrates and herby oils, which he had listed in so much detail. There *had* to be a way.

It was when he overheard a conversation whilst standing in the queue waiting to pay, that Mister Scarab began to smile. He smiled for the first time in days. His smile grew into a grin – which widened into a broad beam – and he felt the beginning of a devious chuckle bubbling up in his throat. So *that* was how the people of the town had been coping without their good doctor and his marvellous assistant! So *that* was where they

106

were getting their medicines from! He had wondered why he hadn't been met with demands and anxieties of patients, once he had left the doctor's house. So *that* was why!

As he handed over the money for three large bags of toffees, Scarab thought how pleasant it would be to take a stroll into the woods. The forest was particularly beautiful at this time of the year, he had heard; the trees, the leaves, the wild flowers. It would be packed full of enjoyable sights and sounds. His mind began to race as he worked through his plan. He and Doctor Klumpet could take a picnic with them and sit quietly amongst the trees, watching and listening. They needn't make a sound. They needn't disturb the comings and goings of the wildlife. They could wait for as long as it took. It would all be *very* interesting.

Who knew *what* they might come across?

ℰↄ

Finnr whistled happily as he made his way along the rope bridge and down the rickety-pickety ladder. He had left his weather-stick at home today to leave his hands free for gathering. Now he delighted in making the ropes and rungs swing so he had to balance carefully, using his tail to assist, like a monkey. Luscinia chirruped, hopped to the edge of their nest-home and dived down low to the forest floor, picking herself up just at the last moment to swoop back up into the air. The tree-troll laughed when he saw her exuberance. She was always the perfect friend for him. Every day, she had accompanied him through the forest to the collection point. Every day, she had helped gather and pack up all that was required for the Big People's ailments and returned with Finnr to deliver them, back at the crate. She was glad to be of assistance and loved to be beside the one who had brought her into the world, under his hat.

As for Finnr, he was joyous in his work! This was all he had ever wanted to be able to do: put into practice all those years of learning and recording. It was proving difficult without his notebook and the thought of it lying in the doctor's house gave him a tight knot in his stomach and nightmares at night, but as always, the break of dawn lifted his spirits. Also, in appreciation of his efforts, occasionally there were little treats left for him to enjoy; tasty, sugar-coated sweetmeats or pretty, sparkling trinkets which he hung in his home to catch the morning light, and sometimes there were pictures drawn by little children to say, 'thank you'. These he valued the most and chuckled over them as he pinned them up inside his nest-home.

He was proud of his knowledge. He was proud of his success. He was particularly proud of his cleverness in dealing with the Big People, without being caught.

This morning, he crowed with pleasure as he scooted through the woodland. Sure enough, there were a couple of medicine requests awaiting him – simple complaints of throat infections and warts. Finnr snatched the paper from the top of the crate and stuffed it into his dungarees.

"Comli Luscinia!" he called. "Ve hab morish vildi floweries tvo findor en speshy mushroomer. Comli fastli, fastli mi dearig!"

The dainty nightingale, flushed with her sky pirouettes and acrobatics, swooped down to the tree-troll's shoulder and the two began to make their way back home. They didn't know that there, the weather-stick had fallen from its propped-up position, knocking and tapping as best it could. They did not notice the clouds beginning to bunch together, cheek-to-cheek. Or a discarded toffee paper being blown by a sudden breeze...

Such was their happiness that they did not see a gorse bush tremble slightly as they passed by.

ℰℭ

A few wild flowers had been picked and special mushrooms selected along the way. Finnr and Luscinia were careful to pick only the flowers which grew in abundance and to take only enough for their medicine. The mushrooms were taken from a patch underneath a tree, where spores had settled in the damp leaves, ready for new growth. The troll checked them carefully; he was very wary of the poisonous varieties. These were safe though, and the perfect size for picking – not too large, not too small. And, of course, Finnr made sure he left some for the fae creatures. All trolls knew the rules of mushroom-picking!

The ingredients were laid out on a dry branch in the centre of the nest-home, whilst the two busied themselves. They whistled, peeped and sang to each other in contented togetherness. It was just as Luscinia was selecting a delicate piece of bronze, hazel bark that she stopped, mid-chatter.

Had she heard something?

The little nightingale cocked her head on one side and listened, her broad tail flattened on the nest floor to hold her perfectly still.

"Luscinia? Wass mattoori?"

The bird didn't answer.

Finnr fell silent and felt the troll hair on the back of his neck prickle. His eyes fell upon the weather-stick lying at an angle. He hadn't left it like that. Why had it moved? Had it been trying to send him a sign?

Then –

– a *creeeeeeak…*

A *crack!*

A rung of the rickety-pickety ladder snapped suddenly and knocked against the tree trunk. *Ker-clack!*

There was a sudden leafy thud and a muffled, *"Oof!"*

Then silence.

Finnr looked at Luscinia. Luscinia looked at Finnr. Whatever could this mean? Neither dared make a sound. Neither dared move. Neither dared breathe.

But something had to be done.

One of them would have to be brave enough to spy out of the nest-hole and see what was going on. They *had* to know if they were safe or not.

With weather-stick in his trembling grasp, the intrepid troll took a tentative step forwards. His nest-home squeaked a little. He halted, mid-stride, and listened once more.

Ker-clack!

Another step – and Finnr reached the entrance to his home. Looking back at Luscinia for encouragement, he poked his nose out first and sniffed, cautiously. Smelling nothing amiss, he dared to take a peep. The rope bridge was swinging slightly, but that could just be the breeze, couldn't it? There was no one on it, not even the usual scampering squirrel using it for a shortcut. The troll peered down the tree trunk. The rickety-pickety ladder was swaying far more than usual and the bottom two rungs appeared to have been broken. The end of it flicked like a lizard's tail, ker-clacking against the tree and then came to rest.

However, there was no one to be seen.

All was secret-silent in the forest once more.

With an uneasiness he couldn't quite shake off, Finnr returned to his medicine-making, eating nothing, and drinking only waterfall water all day. He felt a bit sick.

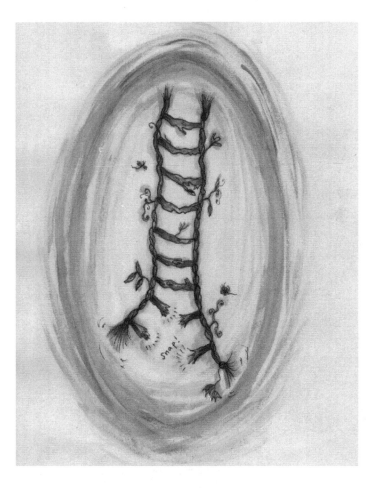

"...and the bottom two rungs appeared to have been broken."

The wooden ladder was cumbersome for Mister Scarab. It was difficult to balance its length as he crept along in the dark, a few hours later. Doctor Klumpet said it was beneath his dignity to carry an object used for labouring and refused to help. Instead he led the way, striding forth with determination, leaving his struggling assistant to follow his thin beam of torchlight as best he could. After a short while, the ladder clattered onto the road, Scarab tripping over it and sprawling face down at the doctor's feet.

"What on earth do you think you're playing at, you fool? You could have knocked me over!"

"Sorry, sorry, Doctor K!" came the wheezing reply. "I feel it's all a bit much for my un-muscley-muscles."

"Nonsense, man! Get on your feet. We haven't even reached the forest again, yet! Shape yourself!"

Once more, the ladder was heaved up and Scarab bore the weight, trudging after the doctor. His breathing became heavy and laboured. The tarmac of the road was left behind them and their feet slipped on damp leaves and wet mud.

"Doctor, Doctor K?"

"Keep your voice down, Scarab! We don't want the troll to hear us coming back!"

"It's just that this ladder is so massively-huge! Why don't we smoky-smoke the little blighter out? Then we wouldn't have to get up there at all."

The doctor came to a halt and turned to look at his scrawny assistant who once more had let the ladder drop. He jabbed at his pocket to locate his bag of toffees, found an exceptionally large one, unwrapped it and sucked hard.

"I mean," continued Mister Scarab, "we could light a fire underneath the tree…" He peered into the dark at the doctor trying to make out the expression on his face. "And the smoke would rise up and…" The slurping was becoming more frantic. Was that a good sign or not? "And the troll would have to come down to us and –"

Mister Scarab could speak no more as Doctor Klumpet suddenly had him by the throat. To his great alarm, he was lifted off the ground so his feet dangled and kicked. Toffee breath filled his face, as Klumpet drew him close to whisper stickily at him.

"How sensible is it to light a fire in the forest, Scarab?"

Scarab did his best to swallow, uncomfortably.

Ah.

Yes.

He hadn't quite thought that one through.

By the time they reached Finnr's tree, Scarab thought his arms were going to drop off. The Big Man's ladder was placed silently at the base, next to the broken rickety-pickety rope one, and the two stood absolutely still, listening. The forest was dark and hushed. All that could be heard was a snoozing snore coming from the tree-nest above them. Pulling out a large sack from beneath his coat, the doctor nodded to his assistant, indicating he should begin to climb. Mister Scarab opened his mouth to complain that his weary arms would not be able to hold on, but realised that the rungs would certainly not support Doctor Klumpet's great weight, and they didn't have another ladder.

Slowly…

slowly…

step – by – step…

rung – by – rung…

Scarab crept up towards Finnr's home. He paused when he reached the top, listening once more. The sound of sweet snoring whistles reached his ears.

Zzzzzzz.

Zzzzzzz.

Zzzzzzz.

With the aid of torchlight shone from below, he found the opening to the nest and thrust his hand inside. He began to fumble around, grappling at the twigs. Where *were* the ingredients kept? They *must* be here somewhere! His hand flapped around, blindly. His fingers poked and pried.

Zzzzzzz.

Eventually, a small bottle fell from a leafy pocket in the wall and Scarab grabbed at it. He threw it down to the waiting doctor who caught it deftly and popped it into his sack. Once more Mister Scarab plunged his hand inside the nest, more roughly this time, in his excitement. The children's letters were ripped, and the precious, dangling trinkets, disturbed. He groped his way around the walls, feeling for pockets and hollows, pulling out jars and pots. One after the other, they tumbled from their tidy keeping places and were cast down to the open sack.

Poke. Prod. Grapple. Grasp. Fumbling here, scrabbling there.

Until, in a sudden *rush* of heart-stopping *terror*, Finnr awoke to see a large spider-hand feeling its way towards him!

115

He gaped in horror and his white whiskers stood up on end in fright, as he gasped and choked, panic gripping his throat.

What was this?

Who was this?

Outraged and screeching like a demented banshee, he leapt to his feet, knocking Luscinia from her perch and out of her deep sleep.

"NAY! NAY!" the troll shouted, trying to stab at the snatching hand with his weather-stick. He stamped and kicked out, violently. "OUTEN MI HOMERIG!" he yelled.

In the mêlée, Luscinia fell. She fell in a rumple of ruffled feathers. But, she fell in a rumple of ruffled feathers, alarmed and shrieking – straight into Scarab's probing grasp!

"MI BEEBEE! NAY! NICS MI BEEBEE!" screamed Finnr in anguish, as the great hand clutched the tiny bird and plucked it out of the nest.

As his assistant almost fell down the ladder, bird in hand, Doctor Klumpet smiled in the darkness. He licked his sticky lips, pink with satisfaction. Perfect!

"Now, troll," he called up the tree. "Throw down all your ingredients at once!" He rubbed his fat hands together in anticipation. "Or your fluffy, little bird friend will be *baked! Mmmm… baked in a tasty pie!*"

"...a large spider-hand feeling its way..."

Chapter Eight

"Don't get mad. Get even."

Like a cat dropping its kill, Mister Scarab passed Luscinia to his master. Klumpet's deep-throated chuckle resounded through the forest, and a chill wind rustled the leaves at his feet.

"Make your demands, Doctor K!" Mister Scarab smirked in the gloom. "It's all exy-excellent! You have the troll in the palmy-palm of your clever handie."

"What I have, Scarab," the doctor replied smugly, "is a plump, juicy birdie in the palm of my handie!"

At these words the Big Man tightened his grip on poor Luscinia who struggled, feebly gasping for air. She managed to turn her head to look imploringly up at Finnr who was hanging onto his rope bridge, anguish and fear causing his old, hairy knees to knock together.

"Mi beebee tweetor!" he cried out in distress. "Pleasor gib meer mi beebee backen. Biggy menor nics eatig mi Luscinia in pyor!"

"Listen to him squawk, Mister Scarab!"

"I'm listeny-listening Doctor K!"

"Do you think he wants something, Mister Scarab?"

"I thinky-think he might, Doctor K!"

There was a pause, as the Big Man waited. Then –

"THROW DOWN YOUR INGREDIENTS, OR THE BIRD GETS IT!"

In an instant, Finnr became absolutely *frantic*. Whatever the cost, he had to protect his tiny friend! He dived back into his nest-home and proceeded to throw out jars and bottles, seeds and flowers. Down fell boxes of powders. Down fell ancient potions and remedies. Down fell elixirs and tonics and cures.

All of Finnr's life-work seemed to unravel as it came cascading down to the forest floor.

"Heer badli menor! Hab mi thingors!" he panted, as he flung out everything he could lay his little troll hands on. "Pleasor gib meer mi tweetor!"

Scarab darted here and there in glee, picking up all the troll's medicines and hurriedly stuffing them into the sack. What a success! Everything they needed without having to buy, forage or make! Now he and the doctor had the troll's notebook *and* ingredients, they were *bound* to be rich. They were going to make their fortunes out of the tree-troll's secrets! All his dreams would come true. Cars, boats, planes. Huge mansion. Private holiday island. All his. Wonderful!

The chaos was all over in a matter of minutes.

Once the sack was stuffed, Klumpet was satisfied and he took a last look at Finnr's desperate face.

"Why, thank you troll," he called up the tree, with a greedy smile. "You are most kind. I'll leave you with this wretched, scrawny scrap and bid you adieu."

119

So saying, he cast the bedraggled body of Luscinia to the ground and beckoned Mister Scarab.

"Not keen on baked birds anyway," he chortled. "All feathers, skin and bone. Give me a bag of toffees any day!"

Carelessly he threw a fat sweet into his gaping mouth and strode off, triumphant. Mister Scarab, sack over his shoulder, scuttled after him. Neither looked back. Neither saw the bag of toffees which had fallen to the forest floor. Neither cared about the pathetic bundle of scruffy feathers which lay amongst the pine needles.

ℰℴ

The next morning whispered its way into the forest.

The dawn chorus had been subdued as only a few birds had roused themselves without Finnr's weather-stick. There was no joyous greeting of the day. There was no celebration. There was no cheerful beginning.

Finnr squatted in the tattered nest, rocking Luscinia in his cupped hands. His hot tears fell upon her closed eyelids and trickled into the ruff of feathers around her tiny, ragged neck. She still breathed shallow bird-breaths, but Finnr knew she was struggling. Snuffling his sobs back, he got to his feet and placed his little baby carefully into his hat; the hat which had so lovingly cradled her egg. He had to get help. His cousin-trolls, Grimhildr and Dotta would know what to do. They would care for her.

Over the next few days, the bell in the forest rang each morning as usual. Notes were left but not collected. The Big People could not understand why. They talked amongst themselves worrying about the situation, but there was nothing more they could do. If the troll did not respond, they did not get help when they were poorly. Simple as that. All they could hope for was that Doctor Klumpet would be working again soon, even if his cures were not as good. After a while, the bell fell silent.

Finnr wanted nothing more to do with the Big People's ailments. They did not concern him now. He had spent a long time trying to clear up his nest-home, but somehow it didn't feel as cosy or safe anymore. In his haste to throw out all his remedies, the hidey-holes had been frantically pulled at and now they were not neat and tidy. Despite his efforts to put things right, twigs lay in disarray still, and the structure of his beautiful tree house was not as strong or comfortable. It looked a wreck. It felt unclean.

Finnr hated it when things were not in order. He couldn't sleep. He couldn't settle. His head pounded with rage when he thought of Doctor Klumpet and his cruel assistant. The injustice of it all made him seethe.

His notebook!

His notebook!

His notebook was not lost; it had been stolen! How could he test and develop new remedies now? All that work! He clenched and unclenched his fists. He ground his gappy teeth together as he tried to make his home special once more.

How dare they?

How dare they do this to him?

How dare they keep his notebook *and* steal his ingredients?

Then Finnr drew a wretched breath from deep within.

How *dare* they harm his dear, little friend?

At the thought of Luscinia, Finnr's eyes welled-up once more. He knew she was in good hands now, staying with Dotta and Grimhildr, but she had suffered so much.

And all because of Doctor Klumpet's greed.

Thinking of the doctor's gluttony, Finnr glanced at the bag of toffees which lay in a crumpled heap in a corner. He had picked them up when the Big Men had left, not wanting the forest floor to be littered, but then he hadn't known what to do with them. He had sniffed them cautiously but they made his stomach churn and he felt quite sick at the manufactured stickiness. Nothing like the natural honey drops Hildi made. Nothing like the sweet-scented berries which grew on bushes up and down the hillside, above the fjord. He wrinkled his nose up at them now. Artificial nastiness. He remembered the doctor's words as he had left: *'Give me a bag of toffees any day!'* How typical of Big People to love something so disgusting!

Then, in the man-made mess of his nest-home, Finnr had an idea.

The idea made him sit upright and blink suddenly. He held his breath and bit his lip to stop himself from shouting out in excitement. His anger lifted immediately and gave way to the rush of another emotion.

An emotion unknown before, to the peaceful tree-troll.

An emotion that came rolling over him in a wash of conviction, even though it was against everything the trolls stood for in the way they led their gentle lives.

It was the thrill of *revenge!*

The idea grew and grew, from a sapling thought to a fully-grown, sturdy plan, each fresh leaf of detail unfurling in greater clarity, until Finnr laughed out loud.

Excellent!

Marvellurg!

That would teach Klumpet to mess with the medicine-maker of the forest!

හ

At first, Scarab was puzzled to find a bag of toffees on the doorstep when he arrived for work, the next day.

How strange.

He picked the bag up and opened it to peer inside. Definitely toffees. And just the sort Doctor Klumpet liked. Scarab looked up and down the road but could see no one. Sealing the bag once more, he entered the house, calling to his employer to announce his arrival.

"Good morning, Doctor K!" he sang brightly, as he threw back the curtains to let in the morning light. It shone onto the table where there were stacks of coins and notes, together with papers showing Klumpet's avaricious adding-up. "Had a good day again yesterday, I see!"

It was true. Since returning with Finnr's ingredients, business had been both brisk and rewarding. Big People had been queuing up as word had got around that the doctor and his assistant were now back in business. The medicines were unusual, but gone was the unpopular gloopy-poop-poop and no one had been given leeches for days. It was evident that the pair had indeed been busy, 'learning new skills and lots of clever stuff', as the note on the doctor's door had declared. So successful were they, that house-calls had been cancelled, and all patients presented themselves at Klumpet's, enabling him to see more people in the time and, of course, make more money. Each person who visited, once the symptoms had been described, waited whilst Doctor Klumpet consulted his notes and Mister Scarab collected and mixed the strangest of ingredients from an odd assortment of bottles and jars, spread out over the table. Each person was charged a fee for the consultation and then a further fee for the medicine, amounting to a large sum – and Doctor Klumpet hadn't even had to leave his house! Money was pouring in.

Mister Scarab handed over the bag of toffees he had found on the doorstep. The doctor's piggy eyes brightened immediately, despite blinking in the sunlight which had suddenly invaded his room.

"Toffees!" he breathed gleefully, stuffing his hand into the bag. "You really are the most excellent assistant, Scarab!"

"Actually, Doctor K," Scarab explained, "I found them on the doorstep. They must be a present for you."

"A present?"

"Indeedy-deedy."

"How splendid! Obviously someone wants to thank me for attending to their needs." A smile and a rub of the hands followed. "Remind me to put up the charges again, Scarab!"

એા

The little bird was responding well to warm troll-love and care. She spent her days and nights resting in a nest-box, specially made by Grimhildr, which had been placed gently in a sunny patch, on the window-ledge of the she-trolls' shack. Dotta was a tender nurse. She watched over her charge without tiring and was rewarded finally, when the nightingale had taken drops of waterfall water from a tiny pipe which had been fashioned from wood. Luscinia's eyes had brightened and her feathers, although still dull, had begun to come together as Dotta helped her to preen them into order. It was just as a small helping of mealworms, forest-ants and berries was being pecked at hesitantly, that a familiar knock sounded at the door.

"Halloo!" a voice called. "Es meer, Hildi!"

Dotta left her patient, happy that she was swallowing without gulping or choking, and let the visitor in with a loving smile.

"Hildi, mi dearig sistoori!" she replied. "Comli, comli en hab nettli tay wit meer."

Grimhildr was called in from milking the goats and together the three sisters sat at the wooden table, enjoying

125

Dotta's tea and the honey buns which Hildi had brought in her basket. She had left her mice at home for once, knowing that there would be very little left if they were given the chance to share the basket and come along for the ride. It was quite often that the three sisters would get together like this. Just as Thom enjoyed the friendship of Hairy Bogley at the water's edge to talk about boats and fishing, or sitting comfortably with Finnr in the forest, sharing porridge, Hildi sought the company of her sister-trolls to chat and laugh with.

Today however, Hildi brought some intriguing – and alarming – news. She had been into the town of the Big People as she did occasionally, to swap some of her hand-crafted water and forest pictures for some tools Thom needed. Hildi did this with great care as she was not happy when Big People were around. She knew a couple of friendly shopkeepers who would trade with her, but most made her unwelcome, since she didn't have money (in true troll fashion). She visited only when she really had to, and always hurried away. This morning, the town had been full of gossip and it had been difficult to reach her lady shopkeeper, without being stopped in the street.

"Biggy Menor shtop u?" questioned Dotta, concerned.

"Yo, yo," replied Hildi, nodding. "Biggy Menor askli foor helpen. Dee fatli doctoori es krankoosh!"

The sister-trolls were puzzled. How could the Big People's doctor be ill? Surely *he* would be the *last* person to get poorly, knowing medicine as he did.

"Dee Biggy Menor askli foor dee foresh troll."

"Ah! Finnr!" Grimhildr and Dotta exclaimed in unison.

126

Of course, all the trolls knew that Finnr had been practising his medicine on the Big People, but as far as they were aware, he was not visiting the town anymore.

"Wass mattoori wit dee doctoori, Hildi?"

Hildi told them all she knew. The doctor had been absolutely fine earlier, eating something called 'toffee' in fact. Then, quite suddenly, he had been taken very ill. At first, he complained of thirst and a dry mouth. When his assistant had given him a drink of water, he had found it almost impossible to swallow – and then difficult to speak. He hid his eyes from the light and claimed there were *two* Mister Scarabs in the room.

"Tvo?" interrupted Dotta.

"Yo, tvo beetloosh menor!"

A few minutes later, when the doctor had flailed his arms about, trying to rid his room of an army of beetle-men in green coats, his assistant had fled into the street, lest he get pummelled mercilessly into a pulp! The doctor seemed to have gone quite mad. The talk of the town was all about his mysterious illness and how Mister Scarab was at a loss to know what to do. When Hildi had turned up, they begged her to tell them where the medicine-troll lived.

"U nics gib secresht, Hildi?" questioned Grimhildr, horrified to think that the Big People might learn where Finnr was.

"Nay! Nay!" replied Hildi. "Im runnig fastli homerig!"

And so she had. Hildi had felt threatened by the Big People's interest in her and she certainly didn't want to tell them where any of the trolls lived, so she had fled. On reaching home, she had calmed herself by making honey buns and had decided to tell her sisters all about it.

The trolls chewed thoughtfully and nursed their steaming mugs of nettle tea.

"Es monkee-monkee, im thinken," commented Dotta at last. "Es soundor liker belladonna tvo meer. En Finnr nics liker dee doctoori."

Hildi's hand flew to her mouth.

"Belladonna? Nay! Finnr? Nay! Nics Finnr wit belladonna. Nics monkee-monkee wit belladonna!"

Dotta looked at Grimhildr for confirmation. The two knew about plants in the forest and which ones made the animals they rescued, ill. The wrong berries eaten and all could be lost. The wrong root unearthed and nibbled, and there would be no chance of survival. Grimhildr nodded gravely. Hildi gasped. Surely not! Belladonna?

Deadly nightshade? The star of the poison plants?

Whatever had Finnr been up to?

ℰᴐ

As he paced up and down the road outside the doctor's house, Mister Scarab began to panic. He couldn't go back inside because his presence seemed to make Klumpet worse; he saw him as an army of beetles and unsurprisingly that caused him great concern. What was happening? How could the doctor be so very ill? What should he do? He couldn't consult the information in Finnr's notebook, as it was in the

"The star of the poison plants?"

house. He couldn't get at the tonics and medicines, as they were there too. In any case, this looked more and more like a type of poisoning and he wasn't sure what the antidote would be. He didn't dare go into the forest alone to find the troll, to ask for help; he might get lost – and he very much doubted that the troll would assist. He swallowed nervously. How long did the doctor have left? How serious was this? Scarab threw his arms in the air and wailed in despair. All his plans! All his scheming for the future! His sports car! His yacht! His private jet! Where would they come from *now*?

He watched disconsolately as some of the Big People went to ring the bell in the forest again. They needed help too. Without the doctor's care, where would they be? They had to try once more, to contact the troll. Scarab sat down in a miserable heap at the side of the road, head in hands.

At the top of his rickety-pickety ladder, Finnr smiled to himself. He heard the incessant clang-clanging of the bell.

He knew his plan was working.

Chapter Nine

"Out of the frying pan... into the fire."

Clang! Clang! Clang!

Reindeer bolted. Squirrels scattered. Foxes covered their ears with their paws and curled up even tighter in their dens. Birds took to their wings in hurried feather-flappings and even the butterflies flitted from their flowers. Tailo and Scratchen heard it and scampered up the dresser to hide in a chipped bowl. Grimo dashed inside and took up guard on the window ledge, eyes round and ears flat back. Hildi looked up and paused in her picture-sticking. Thom heard it, way out on the fjord, in Mistig Vorter. Grimhildr stopped chopping wood when she heard it, and Dotta hurried to reassure the animals in her care. Hairy Bogley, snoozing with Ulf in his cave, heard it, momentarily snorting awake before turning over and dreaming once more.

The last clang of the bell echoed through the trees and then – a hush descended on the forest.

Finnr sat in his nest, listening.

He knew what the sound meant.

The Big People would need him now. Now was the time to make a move. The Big People were without a doctor and they were worried.

Klumpet was ill and Finnr knew why.

He *had* been careful. He had found the *freshest* of the purple, bell-shaped flowers in the shady undergrowth and had gathered their petals cautiously. He did *not* lick his fingers as he searched for the black, shiny berries of perfect ripeness and sweetness. He picked an *exact* number. He had scrabbled around in the soft mulch of the forest floor and pulled out the thick root, despite its white flesh resisting his grip. All had been ground up between two flat stones until the troll had a sticky paste and this he had smeared over each individual toffee, before wrapping them once more in their rustling papers. It had been tricky to work out the correct dosage; Finnr wanted only for Klumpet to become *ill*, not any worse. He thought long and hard about the doctor's height, thinking about how many rungs of his rickety-pickety ladder he had reached when standing, shouting up at him to throw down his pots and bottles. The memory made Finnr wince once more. The Big Man's weight was more difficult to calculate, though. Finnr had no experience of the weight of someone of Doctor Klumpet's proportions and so he guessed as best he could. Once he had completed his work, the medicine-troll washed his hands thoroughly in a waterfall which cascaded into the deep, deep fjord, taking all traces of the deadly poison with it. Finnr had no doubt the toffees would be eaten. He was pretty sure the doctor would not be able to resist such a kind gesture. Klumpet was bound to have worked up quite an appetite after

132

his villainy in the forest. And now, after the insistent ringing of the bell, Finnr knew his plan had worked. He had to time it just right, so that he went to the Big People when they were at their most desperate.

It was just as the tree-troll was packing his hat to go to the town that he heard a *halloo-ing!* Someone was calling out his name in an urgent fashion and tapping at his tree with a noisy stick. Finnr poked his head out of his nest-hole and looked down the trunk. There was Thom, with Tracker at his side. A warm feeling washed over Finnr and he felt a rush of love for his friend.

"Halloo Thom! Im comli fastli!" he answered joyfully, and so saying he grabbed his weather-stick, jammed his hat firmly on his head and slid speedily down his rickety-pickety ladder, with both feet on the side ropes. In less than a minute he had sprung off and grasped Thom's hands in his own. It felt good to have a friend with him after all he had been through.

"Mi dearig frendor, Thom," smiled Finnr, the two trolls touching foreheads before hugging warmly.

"Mi dearig frendor, Finnr," affirmed Thom, and was then straight to the point. "Wass mattoori? Wass happenig wit dee doctoori, Finnr? Hab u mekken monkee-monkee?"

Finnr looked slightly ashamed and more than a little embarrassed at his friend's questioning. With a sigh, he sat down on an old tree stump and beckoned Thom to join him.

He heard how Hildi had been stopped by the Big People. He heard how they had asked for the medicine-troll and how Hildi had run home quickly, worried for her own safety. He heard how Grimhildr and Dotta, still nursing poor little

133

Luscinia, had suspected belladonna poisoning. They had put two and two together and come up with the answer. Finnr.

"Dee doctoori es verisht badli, Thom!"

"Yo, yo, Finnr."

"Dee Biggy Menor hab mi notooris!"

"Yo, yo, Finnr."

A pause. Then a clenching of hairy fists.

"Dee Biggy Menor hurtig mi tweetor."

"Yo, yo, Finnr."

It was clear to Thom that Finnr had been very upset. He had chosen to take his revenge and what was done, was done. It was not for Thom to tell Finnr that what he had done was wrong; what the Big Men had done was wrong too. Thom was not there to judge him. Thom did what all good friends would do. He gave Finnr a manly hug and got to his feet.

"Im goingor wit u," he announced. "Im helpen u wit dee Biggy Menor. Tracker comli tvo."

Finnr broke into a gappy grin of relief! To have Thom, the Warrior Troll, at his side would be wonderful! What lay ahead of him was not easy. He had to risk it, but he was not looking forward to it. This had been his plan and he was determined to carry it out, but it was not without danger. He had to go into the town, face the doctor and demand his notebook. He had to administer the antidote, hope it worked, and then somehow escape, back to his life in the forest. All this would be so much easier with Thom to advise and guide him, watch out for him and help him.

Finnr shook Thom's hand firmly.

"Thanken, thanken, dearig Thom."

134

He was indeed a true and trusted friend.

It was impossible to sneak into the town unseen. Big People were everywhere, like wasps around rotten apples, and many were on the lookout for Finnr. Although they had only a vague notion of his appearance – it had been the stuff of hazy, jonquil dreams – his trollness, and that of Thom, was obvious. Tracker watched fiercely and growled, with hackles raised, when anyone came too close. Bit by bit, a crowd gathered and accompanied the odd little group to the doctor's house. It was clear the Big People were delighted to see Finnr; they *whooped and cheered,* spreading the word quickly. Everyone was relieved to think that help might be at hand for Klumpet's mysterious illness.

Mister Scarab met the two of them.

He was bent and beetle-like as he scuttled to usher them into the doctor's house. Tracker stayed outside; there was no way he was going to enter. His memories of the Big People were all too vivid. He whined a little and pawed at the door, anxious that his beloved Thom had gone inside. The swarm of people buzzed with expectancy, all wanting to get close to the house, jumping to try to get a clear view over each other's heads. The dog began to pace up and down, guarding and waiting with impatience.

Unknown to all was that they had been followed. They had been followed by a smoky-grey cat. Grimo, intrigued by the commotion, had kept his distance. His silent paddy-paws had picked their way nimbly through the forest and with swift skill, through the town. Now, he slipped between the legs of the Big People and jumped onto the window ledge, to peer through a crack in the curtains.

Inside the dimly-lit room, Doctor Klumpet lay sweating, pink and bloated, on an antique pigskin sofa. A runnel of drool spilled from his lower lip as he grunted in an unnatural slumber. Toffee papers were strewn on the floor and the bag lay empty. Mister Scarab looked on anxiously as Finnr made a great play of his examination.

"Can you helpy-help him Mister Troll?" Scarab queried, trying to sound as respectful as possible. "We do hopey-hope you can."

Finnr put his hand on Klumpet's clammy brow and tutted, shaking his head.

Scarab edged a little closer and tugged at Finnr's dungarees, like an annoying child.

"You are such a clever troll! Surely-surely you can do something," he wheedled.

Finnr tapped the doctor's chest with his weather-stick and frowned, pretending to think very deeply.

"You must have some medicine ideary-dears, haven't you?" implored Scarab, becoming increasingly desperate, wringing his hands as his future plans flashed before him.

Finnr fixed the assistant with a very hard stare. He would not be rushed. Of course he knew *exactly* what the problem was! Of course he knew *exactly* how to treat it! But equally, he wanted this shrivelling specimen of a Big Man to realise that

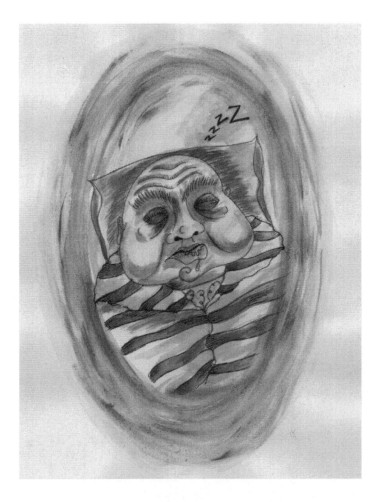

"A runnel of drool spilled from his lower lip…"

the tables were turned. Finnr now held the power! He wanted Scarab to remember how he and the doctor had stolen his belongings and threatened Luscinia. He wanted Mister Scarab to *beg!*

A murmuring began outside.

The gathered throng was becoming restless and more than a little uneasy. What if the troll *didn't* know what was wrong? What if the troll *couldn't* cure the doctor? Where would *that* leave them? Someone rattled at the door handle and Thom heard a sharp bark from Tracker. They had been a while now. He looked at Finnr with real concern. Surely he *did* know what to do? Had he overdone the belladonna? Had he smeared too much on those toffees after all? Why was he taking so long over this?

Scarab could stand it no longer. He lunged at the table where Doctor Klumpet's sheets of adding-up, change and notes were stacked neatly from the day before. He grabbed a few coins, sending the others spinning onto the floor and thrust them at Finnr.

"Here! We'll pay! Take the money!"

The troll did not respond.

"More? You want more?" Scarab snatched up some notes and jabbed them under Finnr's nose.

Still the troll did not respond.

"Take it! Takey-take it! Have as much as you want, but just *do* something!"

Thom stepped forward, in between the Big Man and Finnr. He spoke quietly, making sure he did not use troll-talk so he would be understood.

"We do not want your money. Trolls do not use money. Keep it. We have no interest in it."

Mister Scarab was nonplussed. Who, in this world, did *not* want money? He looked around him, in desperation. What else could he offer? Doctor Klumpet made a strange, animal sort of gurgling noise. His assistant ran to his side and took hold of one flabby hand. He needed the doctor! His face lost its sharpness and began to sag. His lower lip trembled slightly.

"Please," he whispered hoarsely. "Please do something. I beggy-beg you!"

"Ha!" retorted Finnr. At last he had heard the words: *'please'* and *'beg'*!

"Anything!" declared Mister Scarab loudly as the front door gave way to the incessant pushing of the crowd outside, despite Tracker's attempts to keep them at bay. "Tell me what you want! What about a housey-house? Here in the town?"

Finnr was astounded. A house? In the town? Why on earth would he want that? Why would he swap his tumbledown magpie's nest of a tree house, for a boring town house?

Thom had waited long enough. He gestured to Finnr and nodded towards the Big People who were jostling noisily to get inside the room. This situation could get out of control.

Finnr raised his weather-stick and pointed it, threateningly, at Scarab.

"My notebook."

There was a silence. Scarab swallowed an awkward lump in his throat. Then he smiled and bowed his head.

"Anything! Yes, yes of coursey-course!"

In a flash, Finnr whipped off his hat and took out a phial of twinkling elixir. Asking for a glass of water, he put a thumb over the end and shook it vigorously. He then unscrewed the lid and poured one teaspoonful out. Flashes and sparkles lit up the room as he mixed it with the water and presented it to Mister Scarab: *Lively Day-Bright,* the perfect antidote to Deadly Nightshade! A quick whiff of smelling salts was all it took to bring the doctor round and he was given the medicine, speedily.

Klumpet coughed and spluttered. He took a deep breath and swallowed. He burped and retched.

"HOORAY! A BUCKET, QUICK!" the crowd yelled, delighted to see the doctor recovering, even if it was rather unpleasant to watch. The only way to get rid of poison is to get it out of the body – and this Klumpet did, with vigour. Within minutes, he was sitting up, looking a little green but otherwise quite well, enjoying the wafting of Mister Scarab's fanning with a newspaper.

Finnr gathered his weather-stick and phial, and replaced his hat. He turned to address the doctor and his assistant, aware that the assembled Big People would hear what he had to say.

"And so, my notebook, please."

Silence.

"I want my notebook back."

Mister Scarab looked at the doctor. The doctor looked at Mister Scarab. They looked at the group in the room and as one, shrugged their shoulders, palms of their hands spread wide.

"I want my notebook back. You took it from me. It is not yours."

Klumpet blinked and smiled foolishly at the crowd.

"I don't know what he's talking about!"

The crowd began to talk amongst themselves.

"Notebook?"

"What does he mean?"

"The doctor obviously doesn't have any notebook!"

Finnr felt a knot of unease in his stomach. He had not anticipated this; that he would be *lied* to. He had no idea how Big People's minds worked. Of course they had the notebook! Of course they knew what he was talking about! Now the doctor was recovering, they should keep their side of the bargain. That was the plan, wasn't it?

Thom began to look for exits. The room was full. Realisation hit home. Here they were, surrounded by Big People, with no obvious way out.

What had they got themselves into?

Finnr banged the end of his weather-stick on the floor. His expression was determined and angry.

"WHERE IS MY NOTEBOOK? YOU STOLE IT!"

The mass of Big People gasped. Such an accusation! How dare a small troll-man say such a thing? The doctor might not be terribly good at medicine, but he was no thief! Mister Scarab raised his hand and took control of the situation.

"I thinky-think you must be mistaken, Mister Troll. Why ever should the good Doctor take your notebook? It isn't here. Now, I suggest you go on your way, back to your silly troll-folk and leave us to our important, medical work!"

141

There was a hum of talk from the throng. Not everyone was happy to see the troll disappear once more. A voice called out from the back of the group:

"Never mind the notebook, why doesn't he just stay here with you and the Doctor, and work for us?"

"Hear, hear! Good idea!"

"He can work his troll-medicine with you, Klumpet!"

At this suggestion, Finnr gulped. Thom knew it was time to leave. This was all going horribly wrong.

Mister Scarab's eyes became two thin slits as he drummed his fingers on his top lip. This wasn't such a bad idea, actually. If the nuisance-troll actually worked *for* them, instead of *against* them, the people of the town would be very happy to continue to pay him and the doctor! There would be no more trotting through the forest with requests. There would be no more doubts as to Doctor Klumpet's ability. There would be no more threat to their livelihood!

"What do you say to that, troll-man?" he asked, as all listened intently.

"NEVER!" yelled Finnr, as Thom reached to grab his hand. Wildly, they looked for an escape, each pulling at the other in an attempt to flee.

"GET HIM, QUICKLY!" commanded Scarab, and as one, the crowd surged forwards. Huge fingers grappled at Finnr's dungaree straps; hands flailed in the air around them; there were shouts and bellows, shrieks and cries, as all tried to get a grip on Finnr's hairy body. The two trolls ducked and dodged, darted and dived until –

– there was a *great*

growly-snarl

followed by a tremendous

wurr-oof!

And Tracker leapt into the middle of them! The Big People screamed with fear, thinking a forest wolf had somehow entered the room and they scattered as best they could, clawing at the walls, some climbing over others in their attempts to get away.

Thom saw his chance. He tugged Finnr towards the window and flung it open. Pushing the tree-troll out first, Thom then jumped and they ran for their lives, Finnr holding his weather-stick in one hand and his hat in the other. Tracker soon followed and caught up with them, his tongue lolling out of his mouth, as he panted with exertion.

ဆာ

"Oops," thought Grimo as he resumed his position on the doctor's window ledge a few minutes later, "*that* didn't go awfully well!"

The cat groomed himself quietly until all the fuss had died down and everyone had left. The sun was beginning to set and he was just considering returning home for Hildi's smoked fish, when a movement inside the room caught his eye.

Fancy that! Doctor Klumpet appeared to be taking an old notebook out from underneath his bed.

ဆာ

Chapter Ten

"Use a thief to catch a thief..."

The comforting fire in Thom and Hildi's cottage had long since gone out. The hearth, where Finnr had been sleeping, was full of cinders. He shuffled to ease his aching limbs and, absentmindedly stretched out a gentle hand to pet Luscinia. He felt only stone and the wooden floor. No soft, downy feathers and affectionate peck-pecking of greeting. Opening one eye in confusion, the tree-troll remembered then where he was and sat up straight. The blanket Hildi had given him the night before fell from his shoulders and puffed ash into the air. Finnr watched it dance and swirl, catching the sunshine from the open window, like faerie dust. A cool breeze caressed his face and he realised that the day must have begun already.

Sure enough, there was Hildi, quietly feeding Grimo and the mice. Her old feet shuffled about the room as she got on with her jobs. Thom would be home soon from the fjord with cold, fresh water slip-slapping in his bucket and perhaps a fish or two for breakfast.

Finnr thought about the events of the previous day. His idea had not gone to plan and here he was, once more, without his notebook and feeling foolish. He thought about his nest-home but was reluctant to return. It did not seem so welcoming since the Big Men's visit. Without doubt, other Big People would soon find out where he lived and, when the doctor next messed up his work, they would be clamouring for help again. He had been unwise to let fall his guard; he had exposed his troll life to the Big People and now he wasn't safe. What if they decided to kidnap him? What if they forced him to work for the doctor? What if he could never again feel secure in his forest? Finnr heaved a sad sigh, which made Hildi turn around.

"Ah Finnr, u varken oop," she smiled comfortingly. "Comli en sitli foor brekenfasht. Thom comli homerig soonig wit fishen en honig."

Just as Hildi said, as soon as Finnr had taken his seat at the table, in strode Thom, smiling broadly at them both.

"Dee sonnerig es marvellurg todagen! Mi buzzors mekken gooshty honig foor eatig dis morgy."

Within minutes, they were all tucking in, Finnr encouraged to eat well, by the tasty food placed lovingly in front of him. As they ate, inevitably the conversation was of the missing notebook. Hildi and Thom tried hard to encourage Finnr to give it up – to continue trying to retrieve it would be madness, surely. He had escaped narrowly, twice already, and to risk another visit to the Big People would be reckless in the extreme. In addition, none of them knew where the doctor kept it. They couldn't demand it back; that had failed already. They couldn't ransack his house; they would definitely be caught in the act. There seemed to be nothing else for it: Finnr would have to accept its loss.

However, as the three trolls were discussing the situation, their attention was drawn to Grimo. He was making a complete nuisance of himself, which was out of character. Normally at this time of the morning, he would be outside lazing in the sunshine or stalking forest mice. Today though, he was howling and pacing backwards and forwards between the table and Thom and Hildi's bed.

"Wass mattoori wit dee pussor dis morgy?" Thom asked, trying to push Grimo away with one hairy foot. "Shoo-shoo littelor pussor! Ve eatig oor brekenfasht."

Grimo did not shoo. He sat down and began to wash his whiskers, waiting for the conversation to continue. As soon as he heard them mention the notebook, he howled again.

"Grimo! U musten shh! Ve chattoori."

Grimo then mewed sweetly and tapped Thom's leg.

Once more, the cat was pushed away.

This time he turned, howled long and low, and made a mad dash for Hildi and Thom's bed. The trolls looked up from their food in surprise. Whatever *was* the matter with the cat today? When he found he was not being followed, Grimo returned to the table and waited, tail flicking with impatience.

"Mi notoori bookor es…" Finnr continued, but stopped mid-sentence, as a sudden shout came from Thom.

"GRIMO! NAY!"

On hearing the word 'notebook' again, the cat had decided the only thing for it was to use his claws – delicately – on Thom. Once more, having got the trolls' attention, the cat dashed off towards the bed. Thom drew back his chair, feeling cross at the interruption. The wooden legs scraped on the floor and Grimo heard determined troll footsteps approaching. It was just when Thom was about to grab the cat by the scruff of

"Grimo then mewed sweetly and tapped Thom's leg."

the neck to throw him outside, that Grimo finally made himself understood. He scratched and scrabbled at the mat under their little bed and then mewed back towards Finnr. Thom stopped in his tracks.

"Grimo?" questioned Hildi from the kitchen table, looking then to Finnr. "Dee notoori bookor?"

Mew.

"Biggy Menor hab notoori bookor?"

Mew. Mew.

"Dee bookor es wit Doctoori Klumpi-Pumpet, yo?"

Again, Grimo mewed and plucked his claws at the mat. He padded quickly to Finnr, prooped up against his legs and returned to the floor beneath the bed. Thom looked at Hildi. Hildi looked at Thom. They both looked at Finnr.

Was this possible?

Had the cat just told them where the notebook was kept?

Under Klumpi-Pumpet's bed?

This was quite astonishing. How did Grimo know where the notebook was? Gently they asked the cat if they were right; if this was what he meant. There was no doubt as to the response. Grimo began to purr, furiously, and produced his best curly-cat smile. Satisfied at last, he jumped up onto the patchwork quilt and began to lick the fur on his front paws, ready to settle into a well-earned sleep.

Leave these things to cats, he thought, feeling rather superior. *They know a thing or two!*

Over the rest of the morning, Thom did a lot of thinking. It was no good expecting Finnr to come up with a plan. It was clear that planning was not his strength. The trolls had two choices, of course. One was to leave things well alone and not risk further danger. The other was to try once more to retrieve the notebook. Obviously, the easier of the two options was to do nothing. Thom considered this for a moment, but then sighed and shook his head. He knew Finnr would never rest – and possibly never feel completely happy again – without his notebook. There was the moral issue too. It had been very wrong of the Big Men to keep that which did not belong to them. It had been very wrong of them to demand Finnr's ingredients. It had been *dreadful* of them to use poor Luscinia to get their own way.

Thom shuddered quietly.

Also, until the matter was settled once and for all, none of them would feel completely safe living in the forest. Unwittingly, Finnr's meddling with the Big People had made contact none of the trolls wanted. If only they could turn the cuckoo clock back!

There was nothing for it, then. If they wanted to be rid of this problem, the notebook would have to be found and brought back, so everything could return to how it was before. But, this was far from easy. The doctor would be using the notebook during the day and his house would have visitor after visitor until the evening, so there was no way it would be possible to gain entry without being seen. During the night, if Grimo was right, the notebook would be under the doctor's bed... and *in* bed was exactly where the *doctor* would be...

149

Thom chewed a piece of liquorice root, grinding it thoughtfully between his teeth. The problem of Finnr's spoiled home would also have to be resolved.

Announcing he would be back soon, Thom patted his thigh encouragingly at Tracker. Troll and dog left the cottage, closing the door quietly.

ℰℐ

Hairy Bogley was flat on his back, snoring of course. His home-cave sounded as if a hibernating bear was tucked up inside it. Little Ulf was also asleep, seemingly oblivious to the growly rumbling of his uncle which filled the damp air. A swirling spiral of smoke rose from the smouldering heap of charcoal, which still offered a little warmth, and there were discarded crumbs of their midnight feast scattered over the stony floor. Thom smiled to himself. The whiskery baddie was still bogling at night, then! Perfect.

For years now, Hairy Bogley had visited the garages, sheds and outhouses of the Big People, taking odd items of interest. For a long, long time, Thom and the other forest trolls had known nothing of his night-time adventures, since the bogler lived a hermit's life, tucked away in his home-cave. It was only when his little nephew, Ulf, had come to learn how to be an apprentice, that certain events had exposed Hairy Bogley's lifestyle. It was high-risk, but fun and Hairy didn't intend to change his ways. The items bogled were always put to good, if unconventional, use: an old, discarded pan became a necessary cave-potty; kitchen tongs became useful toenail clippers; a screwdriver was invaluable as a back-scratcher. So, whilst the other trolls were not particularly happy about the situation, they accepted that Hairy Bogley was probably not doing any real harm and turned a blind eye. Now Thom hoped his skills would be of real use.

However, this was no ordinary bogling job.

Usually, Hairy Bogley chose to poke around places where there were no Big People. *Usually*, garages, sheds and outhouses were closed for the night. *Usually*, he could come and go without difficulty.

Usually.

It was going to be an altogether different situation this time. Hairy Bogley would have to enter the doctor's house at night, find his bedroom and scrabble about under the bed, when the doctor was actually there! *In bed!*

Thom swallowed. He had to think of a plan...

... and it *had* to work.

They had waited into the night.

Hildi had insisted they had warming mugs of herb soup and hunks of rye bread before they left, so that they would feel strong and fearless. She had kissed them all as they had departed and she was now sitting by the fire, holding Finnr's hat. His weather-stick lay at her feet.

The three intrepid trolls approached the town, cautiously. Hairy Bogley looked up at the moon in the inky-black sky and considered its position. It must be after midnight.

The perfect time for bogling!

Most Big People would be fast asleep, dreaming their Big People dreams of money and work. Little children would be smiling sweetly, dreaming their Little People dreams of scoring goals and finding faeries. Houses would be locked; dogs would be chained up for the night; cats would be out prowling, looking for rats and mice, not in the least interested in three odd-looking visitors creeping through the streets.

The bogler nudged Thom and pulled at Finnr's sleeve. He pointed up at the moon and grinned his best bogley grin. Giving the other two the thumbs-up, Hairy slipped off ahead to find a bush in the doctor's garden, near the door, where he could hide. Thom and Finnr watched him go and soon he disappeared into the darkness. For the umpteenth time, Thom thought through his plan. He had a Big Man's bogled overcoat folded over his arm. Finnr had Thom's bucket gripped tightly in his hairy hand. If Hairy Bogley was quick, this might just work...

Thom looked up at the cool, silver moon swathed in gossamer Will-o'-the-wisp, and breathed a quiet, troll prayer.

"Dearig moonish, es Thom heer. U shineror wit angelicor kissigs. Helpen oos, dis nachtor. Helpen oos findor dee notoori bookor en gib oos fastli leggors foor runnig homerig saftoosh. Thanken, thanken mi dearig moonish."

Finnr listened in the dark and nodded his head earnestly, to every word.

"Thanken, thanken moonish," he whispered, his eyes reflecting the bright orb. And then he added, "Im lovelor u."

℘

Doctor Klumpet was not impressed to be woken up in the middle of the night. He gruffled into his pillow when he was roused by the first knock at his door, hoping whoever it was would take their leave without further disturbance of his sleep. However, there came a second knocking, this time louder and more insistent.

"SCARAB!" Klumpet shouted. "GET THE DOOR, BLAST YOU!"

And then, with a disgruntled *humph*, the doctor remembered that Mister Scarab was at home for the night and in fact, had left some time ago.

The knocking came again.

KNOCK! KNOCK! KNOCK!

And then a *rat-a-tat-tat!*

There was nothing for it. He would have to leave his crumple of sweaty bedding and answer.

A shaft of light came from the hallway and cast a shadow of the figure on the doorstep, down the path. Thom shuffled a little, hoping his grip on Finnr's ankles would hold. Finnr swayed slightly on Thom's shoulders as he did so. He felt slightly sick. How did these Big People cope with being so tall? It was necessary to appear as tall as a Big Man so the doctor would not realise it was a troll at the door, but this circus act was difficult to maintain for more than a few minutes. The long overcoat Hairy Bogley had given them reached Thom's feet and covered them both well, although Thom had to be extra careful not to tread on the hem, otherwise all would be lost. As the doctor's rotund figure approached the door, Finnr swept the bucket up and put it swiftly on his head, hiding his troll features.

So, Doctor Klumpet flung open the door to a very strange sight: a tall man in a long overcoat, with a bucket which appeared to be stuck on his head.

"What's going on?" the doctor questioned as he peered, blinking, into the dark. "Who on earth are *you*?"

Finnr made a muffled noise inside the bucket. It echoed round and made his ears hurt. As planned, Thom took a couple of steps back, away from the door. The doctor advanced two steps, drawing his dressing gown cord around his middle as he did so.

There was enough of a gap behind him now, for someone small to nip inside unnoticed. Someone small and bogler-ish, perhaps.

"Come here, man!" Doctor Klumpet demanded, feeling irritated. It was bad enough being woken up, but now to see what appeared to be a fool with a bucket stuck on his head, making no sense at all when questioned, and stepping backwards away from him, was really, *really* annoying. "Do you want my help or not?"

Once more, Finnr made a noise from inside the bucket, trying to sound more urgent this time and raised his hands as if trying to take it off. The doctor took another step towards him.

"...a tall man in a long overcoat, with a bucket..."

"Stuck, is it? It'll cost you dear at this time of the night! Stand still, man! How can I help you if you keep stepping back from me?" Klumpet grumbled, trying to fumble with the bucket.

Finnr's forehead began to break out in a sweat. It was hot inside the bucket and the overcoat weighed heavily on his shoulders. The effort of balancing on Thom was tiring and Thom's hands kept slipping from around his ankles. How long would Hairy Bogley need?

How long could they keep this up?

Hairy Bogley was frantic. Getting into the house had been simple. He had watched from the bushes and had seen his opportunity to slip inside, when Mister Bucket-Head took a couple of steps back. He had found the doctor's bedroom quickly; the door was open and the bedside lamp switched on. Without wasting a second, he had bogled under the bed, expecting to put his grimy hands on the notebook straight away. That was the plan – then a quick exit before the doorstep-trolls' disguise was uncovered – but where was it?

Where *was* the notebook?

Hairy's expert hands felt underneath the bed. It was dusty and his nails filled with grit from years of dirty feet. Dried-up spiders, all crinkly legs and hairs, brushed against his fingers.

Where *was* the notebook?

"Fastli, fastli Hairy!" the troll muttered to himself. "Fastli tvo findor dee bookor!"

There were muffled voices from outside. Hairy Bogley couldn't make out what was being said, but he could hear the tone and it didn't sound good. He had to hurry. Where could the notebook be? Was Grimo wrong after all?

"Moonish, helpen meer, pleasor!" the bogler appealed in desperation. "Im needen helpen heer!"

A shout was heard from the doorstep.

"TROLLS? YOU TWO *AGAIN*?"

There was a clang as the bucket fell to the ground.

Hairy's fingers slipped over the floor, fumbling and flapping. There were more shouts from outside. The doctor was shouting for Mister Scarab. He was shouting for help. He was shouting for the townspeople to wake up!

Just as Hairy was about to give up and make his escape as best he could, the moonlight shone brightly as clouds shifted away. A beam shone through a chink in the curtains and fell directly upon a floorboard. A floorboard with a small hole in it. A hole small enough not to be noticed before, but large enough for a finger to poke through...

Hairy Bogley lifted the floorboard in a trice.

And there was the notebook!

It was squirreled away under the loose floorboard, amongst the dust and cobwebs!

Snatching it up in relief, the bogler dashed to the window. There was no way he could risk going out of the door, with all the noise that was going on. He would have to leave Finnr and Thom to cope by themselves. With a skilful flick of the catch, an invigorating draught of night air blew against his hot cheeks and in a flash of bogler expertise, he vanished into the night.

Chapter Eleven

"A friend in need..."

"SCARAB! MISTER SCARAB! SOMEONE! ANYONE! HELP ME! TROLLS ARE ON THE LOOSE!"

Doctor Klumpet was absolutely beside himself with rage. His face was bright red and his eyes were bulging.

"TRICKING ME IN THE NIGHT, THEY ARE! HELP! COME QUICKLY, SOMEONE! THIEVES! THIEVES, I SAY!"

Klumpet kicked clumsily at the fallen bucket, as he gave chase. His dressing gown flapped open and his slippers slopped, making his lumbering figure stagger and curse. With outspread hands and heavy thudding feet, he tried his best to follow the fleeing trolls, drawing breath whenever he could, to bawl for help. He was unused to exertion of course, and the effort of trying to run as well as shout, made him wheeze and cough. Spluttering, the Doctor had to stop for a moment, to gasp and fasten the dressing gown cord around his flabby middle.

The second their charade had been discovered, Finnr had flown into a panic. The bucket had clanged onto the path and Finnr had jumped down from Thom's shoulders, eager to make their getaway. In his haste, he had landed badly, pulling Thom down with him in an awkward heap of overcoat and twisted troll arms and legs. They scrabbled about, clutching and tugging at each other, trying to fight their way out. Neither had any idea where Hairy Bogley was, or if he had been successful – and neither had time to worry at this stage. All they could think of was how to escape before Klumpet grabbed them. With a sudden wrench at the buttons, the overcoat released them and, holding hairy hands tightly, they set off at last. They ran wildly through the streets, hearts pumping hard, trying desperately to remember their way back to the forest.

Lights were switched on in the town. Doors and windows were banged open. Big Men shouted. Big dogs barked. Some hounds were set free from their chains and they raced around in excitement. Fancy having a party in the middle of the night! Their owners bawled commands:

"DOWN BOY, DOWN!"

"COME HERE, STUPID DOG!"

"GO FETCH!"

"FETCH THE TROLLS!"

"GET THEM, QUICKLY!"

Speedily, the dogs picked up the troll scent from the doctor's door and they capered off, eager to seize their quarry. The Big People clutched torches and followed in quick pursuit. Not *one* of them understood what had happened at the doctor's house. Not one of them asked – but that didn't seem to matter, caught up as they were in the frenzy of a hysterical mob. Some were brandishing sticks like clubs; some had garden rakes, all sharp, pointed prongs; some had rolling pins to bash with. Mister Scarab followed on behind, shaking his fist in the air,

"...the dogs picked up the troll scent..."

but he was torn between assisting Klumpet and wanting to catch the trolls.

"Doctor K!" he gasped, slowing his pace so the doctor could catch up. "Are you alrighty-right?"

"They came back, Scarab!" fumed Doctor Klumpet. "The two of them knocked at my door to get me out of my bed, with some ridiculous pantomime involving a bucket! I have no idea what they were playing at!"

"What did they say, Doctor K?"

"That was just it, Scarab. They didn't say *anything* except sort of, 'Mmmpf, mmmpf, mmmpf!' The bucket was stuck on his head, you see!"

"Did you get it off?"

"Of course I did, you fool! How else did I know it was them?" Doctor Klumpet thought for a second, casting his mind back. "It came off rather easily actually, Scarab. In fact, blast! Now I come to think of it, it wasn't stuck at all!"

At this, Mister Scarab stopped in his tracks.

"It wasn't stickety-stuck, Doctor K?"

They were obviously missing a trick, here. The two troublesome trolls had returned, risked being caught and fooled the good doctor into thinking they needed help, when they quite clearly didn't. Whatever could be their motive? Scarab turned to Klumpet, his face suddenly pale.

"The notebook!" he gulped.

Klumpet looked aghast. He could think of no reply.

"Noooooooo! Don't tell me they've got it! You didn't leave the doory-door open did you, Doctor K?"

Hairy Bogley used his practised bogling skills to nip through the backstreets. He scurried up alleyways and scampered down ginnels; he bounded over hedges like a March hare and squeezed under gates like a weasel. He had escaped the shouts and the pounding feet, although he could hear them and he knew full well what was going on. Somewhat breathless, he came to a halt at the edge of the forest and looked back at the houses. The hair on the back of his neck prickled at the sound of the baying hounds. This was terrible! It would be dreadful to leave his friends in such danger. Trolls always, *always,* looked after each other and would *never* put themselves first. He knew Thom and Finnr would be terrified. They were not like him.

Hairy Bogley thrilled at the thought of risk. He delighted in getting one over the Big People and if it made them wild with anger, so much the better! Because of his night-time bogling, Hairy was nimble and quick. He knew short cuts and a variety of routes through the town. He could dodge and duck and dive and weave. He could throw dogs off his scent by jumping up onto a roof or by choosing to wade through a river. He could fling them a stolen bone, or sprinkle pepper behind him. Or simply stand up to them and *eyeball* them. He knew all the bogling tricks in the book.

But Thom and Finnr knew none of this. All they knew was how to run. Run as fast as their little, hairy troll legs could carry them. Hairy Bogley could hardly return to Hildi, with the notebook, but no Thom or Finnr. That would never do.

He decided to double back. If he was swift he could locate his friends and lead them away from the usual roads, through troll pathways to safety. So, holding the precious notebook tightly in his grimy hand, the bogler turned and made his way back, towards the dangerous hullabaloo of the town.

No more than a few panic-stricken minutes passed, before Hairy saw them. There was Finnr, galloping wildly, white whiskers blowing. There was Thom, panting heavily, trying to keep up. Finnr was the more agile of the two because he was used to swinging down from his nest-home and climbing up his rickety-pickety ladder. However, he was also the oldest and couldn't keep up the running for long. Thom, whilst strong from rowing on the fjord and wielding his axe when chopping wood, was not so lithe on his feet. The dogs appeared to be snapping at their heels. It was clear to Hairy Bogley they were going to be in serious trouble without his help.

With a strident: *"Hoo-hoo-hoo! Shtop en shtay!"* the bogler burst out from a dark corner of a street, just as Thom and Finnr reached it. He took the dogs quite unawares. They cowered suddenly, hackles raised and snarling. This strange troll, standing full-square before them, was not like the others who fled like excited rabbits. This strange troll fixed them with his beady eyes and looked as if he meant business. The dogs growled but stayed exactly where they were.

"Dis veg, mi frendors! Fastli, fastli!"

Flourishing the notebook high above his head so Finnr and Thom could see it, Hairy indicated a tiny, shadowy

164

passage to their left. He knew it would lead, winding up and down through a cobbled difficult route, straight to the welcome secrecy of the forest. The Big People would be in a frightful crush if they tried to follow them.

Sure enough, as the trolls switched direction and hurried down the passage, the chasing mob skidded to an unexpected halt and bunched up at the entrance, shoving and pushing. The dogs whined and tried their best to avoid the sharp sticks and kicking boots. As they jostled with one another to get some space, one Big Man shouted:

"LOOK! THERE! WHAT'S THAT TROLL WAVING IN THE AIR?"

"HE'S GOT A NOTEBOOK!"

The Big Men squashed together, trying to peer ahead. As they squinted and elbowed each other at the narrow opening, they managed a glimpse of the trolls – and one clearly had a notebook, held high above his head.

And then, they understood.

"SO THERE *WAS* A NOTEBOOK AFTER ALL!"

"That's what they were asking for, when they cured Klumpet of his mysterious illness!"

"The Doctor must have had it all along!"

"So the trolls came back to get it!"

The discussion became heated as the people became more and more angry. The doctor had told them he didn't have the troll's notebook. He had claimed to know nothing about it. He had lied to them all!

It was just at this point that Mister Scarab and Doctor Klumpet caught up. They rushed round the corner in the road and ploughed into the group with an unexpected wallop! Klumpet was furious.

"WHY ON EARTH HAVE YOU ALL STOPPED?" he bellowed, spit flying from his lips. "CAN'T YOU SEE THEY ARE GETTING AWAY?"

As one, the crowd turned around to face the doctor and his lackey. Mister Scarab felt an uncomfortable drop in his guts. He took a cautious step back. This didn't look good. Not good at all.

A horrible silence fell.

The silence was far more threatening than all the shouting had been.

"WELL? Don't just stand there staring at me!" Klumpet blathered. "GO GET THEM!" He waggled a fat finger in the direction of the vanishing trolls.

There was a shuffling of feet and a murmuring amongst the Big People. Some of the dogs whimpered and slipped away, tails between their legs. This party had not turned out to be as much fun as they had thought it would.

A cough sounded and there was a push from the back of the crowd. Mister Colic took it upon himself to be the first to speak.

"The trolls have got a notebook, Doctor Klumpet," he stated, quietly. "We think they got it from your house tonight. Are we wrong? Have we made a mistake?"

"ARE YOU WRONG?" exploded Klumpet, playing for time. "ARE YOU WRONG, YOU ASK?"

Scarab stepped forwards and murmured to the doctor, anxious that they shouldn't anger the mob further.

"Doctor K! Shhh! Calmy-calm yourself, please! Its clear your patients have been *seeing* things; a sort of night-time delirium, if you will. If you explain that there has been some mistake, that they are *not well*, perhaps they will all go home quietly."

Mister Colic, standing at the front, heard the suggestion and was quick to react.

"Oh no! No, no, no, no, no! Don't you try to tell us we're seeing things! How can we all think we have seen the same thing if it wasn't there? There definitely *was* a notebook in the troll's hand and we think it might have come from *your* house." The Big Man paused. "What we're asking is: *did it?*"

Doctor Klumpet was not one to be challenged.

"How do I know where the fool troll got it from?" he retorted. "All I know is that two trolls came knocking at my door in the middle of the night, with mischief afoot, and I am calling upon all of you to help me for once." He warmed to his theme and drew himself up, proudly. "You seem to forget how often I have helped all of you in your times of need. Now stop wasting any more time and CATCH THE TROLLS!"

Mister Scarab winced as the doctor shouted once more. He tugged at Klumpet's sleeve and tried to salvage what he could of the situation, before it got entirely out of hand.

"Doctor K!" he hissed urgently. "Don't make them more cross. I think – "

"Don't make them more cross?" Klumpet responded, without keeping his voice down. "Don't make *them* more *cross?* I think you forget whose side you are on in this, Scarab. And what's more, I think you forget who pays your wages!"

167

The crowd was becoming restless. It was clear that the doctor was not going to answer Mister Colic properly. They began to wonder why they had got out of bed at all, this cold night. Exactly *why* had they run out of their houses, in their pyjamas, with torches and dogs? Why had they rushed to do the doctor's bidding without question?

"You're not going to answer, are you?" a strident voice called out. "It's clear you don't want to admit it!" Madam Septicus had obviously heard enough. She turned to the others around her and spoke loudly.

"When the troll was asked to come to cure the doctor here, he did just that. Remember how he requested his notebook and Mister Scarab replied: 'Of coursey-course!'"

The crowd mumbled in agreement. Many of them had been there at the time.

"And then," continued Madam Septicus, "when the doctor was restored to health, the troll asked for his notebook again."

Once more, the crowd agreed. There was much nodding of heads and tut-tutting amongst them.

"Well, even if you don't remember, dear Doctor Klumpet, we do! You and Mister Scarab pretended you knew nothing of any notebook. You both shook your heads and denied all knowledge!" The Big Woman drew a deep breath. Her cheeks were turning rather pink and her voice shook a little with rising anger. "I'm sorry to have to say this, Doctor Klumpet," she announced, "but you are a LIAR!"

Klumpet looked shocked. He blinked his eyes as if he had been stung. Mister Scarab pulled once more at his sleeve and indicated as best he could that they should, perhaps, move away from the rabble.

"Not only that!" Madam Septicus spat. "You have robbed us of money by pretending you knew how to cure our ailments. You have needed the help of a troll! You have stolen his notebook to further your own ends. Now you have ruined our chance to have the expert help of that troll when we need it! In short, Klumpet (for I no longer call you 'Doctor'), in short, you are not only a liar – but also a THIEF!"

"A TRICKSTER!"

"A SCOUNDREL!"

"A CHARLATAN!"

The throng began to move towards the doctor and his assistant. Angry shouts filled the air. Fists were shaken and growling threats were made. Klumpet and Scarab took a few steps back, concern growing quickly into alarm, and then alarm billowing quickly into fear. How had this happened? How had their plans gone so disastrously wrong?

Fear then gave way to panic.

How fast could they make it home?

Klumpet took another step backwards. Beads of sweat had broken out on his brow and his hands were clammy. He swallowed although his mouth was dry. Turning to Mister Scarab, he began to suck one plump thumb for comfort.

"I don't suppose you've got any toffees have you, Scarab?" he began to blub.

Chapter Twelve

"Home is where the heart is."

As the sun rose, light crept through chinks in the red and white checked curtains of Hildi's kitchen, spreading its fingers slowly over the neatly-swept floor...

... to Finnr's sleeping face. His eyes were closed and he wore the tranquil expression of one at peace with the world. Clasped to his chest was an old, leather-bound notebook, each ivory parchment page still holding precious memories and a lifetime's work. Finnr's heartbeat embraced each word as he dreamed his way through the charcoal notes and feather quill records.

Reunited.

At last.

And, nestled in the crook of his curled-up knees, was a little nightingale, all tucked up, with beak deep in her fluffed feathers. Trills and tweets and warbles and whistles danced in her little bird-dreams, as she flitted happily through the forest with her beloved tree-troll.

Reunited.

At last.

The cuckoo clock had not been wound up that morning to enable the visitors to get some proper sleep. Too many nights had been spent fretting and feverish. Too many days had been spent in anguish and anxiety. Now the healing balm of a soothing slumber was just what both of them needed, and so all was hushed and still in the little cottage. There was a wooden plate on the table, piled high with smoked fish, goat's cheese and rye bread. A small dish had been filled with nuts and berries from the woods. Thom's best summer honey glistened, golden, in a pot, and dried nettle leaves were waiting for the making of tea. Grimo was sunning himself outside and the mice were snoring sweetly on the dresser.

All was calm.

All was peaceful.

All was quiet.

૪૭

Bang! Bash!
Ping! Plop! Plunk!
Crack! Clang!
Eek!
Whack! Wham!
Clatter! Clunk! Crunch!
Ouch!
The other trolls, meanwhile, were busy. Very busy.
Thud! Thump! Twang!
Snip! Smack!
Rattle!
Ow!

Building a new tree house certainly was a team effort.

Thom had been determined to put all things right. Retrieving the notebook had been the main problem, but he knew also that Finnr would never feel safe in his old nesthome again. Just now he was staying with his loyal, loving friends, but he would never feel *truly* happy until he resumed his life amongst the trees and birds. There was only one solution: build a new home for Finnr. A new home, further into the forest, where the Big People dared not venture. A new home, deep in the trees, where Finnr would be out of harm's way and free to live the life he loved.

A secret, surprise new home!

As soon as Thom had thought of the idea, he couldn't wait to put it into practice. To this end, two sturdy, tall trees had been selected. They grew next to each other and were of similar height and girth. A higgledy-piggledy shack was put together, hastily using the strongest of the branches for support. Finnr's rope bridge had been removed and was fixed between the two trees, Thom holding one end and Hairy Bogley the other, whilst little Ulf acted as builder's mate and knocked pegs into the wood to secure it. Unknown to Finnr, his rickety-pickety ladder had been dismantled and repaired. Now it was attached to one of the trees with many loud bangings and the occasional throbbing thumb. Any tools that were needed had been bogled by you-know-who, then fetched and carried on demand by Tracker, all wagging tail and lolling tongue. The trolls worked tirelessly, directed by Thom and sustained by Hildi and Dotta, who provided ample, tasty refreshments and cheery calls of encouragement.

172

Clank!
Knock!
Ugh!
Boing! Bong! Boink!

Thom's wood-chopping strength was used to the full as his axe swung to split and shape fallen, forest timber. Ulf gathered the logs and dragged them to Grimhildr, who grinned with satisfaction as she fashioned storage boxes and a bed, with skilful hands. The furniture was then hauled up the rickety-pickety ladder, by means of ropes and pulleys, each troll helping the other, all as keen as Thom to see a job well-done.

Hairy Bogley was dispatched to Finnr's old nest then, to collect all the remaining belongings. Into Herbie Poshtig went leftover dried flowers, seeds and charcoal. He found the soft blanket which Finnr used to snuggle up in, plucked as many feathers as he could from corners and the floor, and hurried back to the new home. The storage boxes were used for all the bits and bobs, whilst Dotta and Hildi made up the bed with a new feather pillow and mattress, a luxury never before enjoyed by Finnr, and lovingly floofed the blanket on top. There was even a twig hook for his green, floppy hat. As a final touch, Hairy left a present: a new notebook he had bogled especially for the occasion. Perhaps Finnr could use it to record birdsongs, or recipes for flower syrups – geranium was always a favourite – or as a diary of his days in the new nest.

Just as dusk fell, the trolls finished.
Phew!

Their arms and legs ached. They were hot and dirty and exhausted. They looked at the tree house in the woods.

It was spectacular.

Finnr had spent a happy day with Luscinia. They had both woken late in the morning and eaten a hearty breakfast, before pottering about, chattering and whistling songs to each other. Neither was aware of the special project going on in the woods. Neither knew of the excitement which was to come, the following day. Finnr assumed Thom was out on the fjord, fishing in Mistig Vorter, and that Hildi was busy mushroom-picking or visiting her sisters. By the time evening came though, the cottage was filled with smoky fire and cooking smells, happy conversation and laughter. Thom and Hildi did not say anything about their day's work with Hairy Bogley, Ulf, Grimhildr and Dotta. Tracker snoozed contentedly underneath the table and Luscinia was tucked up in a corner of the hearth. As the moon rose, high over the trees, the three trolls sat in companionable silence, munching toasted acorns in quiet contemplation. Eventually, Thom cleared his throat and got to his feet. He rubbed his tired eyes and announced he was off to bed.

"Gooshty nachtor mi dearigs," he smiled at Finnr and Hildi. "Im verisht shleepish. In morgy ve varken oop en mekken happli fonnerig in foresh." He tapped Finnr's shoulder in affection and winked at Hildi. He knew it was going to be a big day for Finnr, tomorrow.

He couldn't wait for the morning to come.

ॐ

Peep! Peep! Toowip! Tooweep!

Dotta was at the door, bright and early, playing troll-music on her pipes. Grimhildr was standing beside her, a basket of russet apples in her hand. Luscinia had woken at dawn and flown through an open window into the forest, to join the other birds, leaving the trolls to busy themselves ahead of the day. As Hildi flung open the door to greet her sisters, she could barely contain her excitement.

"Halloo!" she beamed. "Oor speshy secresht es todagen! Comli, comli en hab littelor drinkoosh wit oos." The two entered the house and hugged Thom and Finnr. Tracker leapt around, excited to have company so early in the morning. Troll-Cherry Wine was poured and passed around. Just as they were about to raise their small mugs in a cheerful toast, a *tappety-tap-tap* was heard at the open door and there stood Hairy Bogley and Ulf.

"Halloo mi dearig frendors!" Thom called to them from the kitchen. "Comli!"

Once more, Troll-Cherry Wine was poured and mugs raised. Finnr hadn't any inkling of what was being celebrated but he was *so* glad to see all his friends together. He felt warm inside. His tweetor was safely with him again. He had his

175

notebook back. He was with those who loved him. He grinned his best gappy grin and felt happier than ever.

"Im happli troll!" he laughed. "Happli, happli!"

Then, just as they were about to clink mugs, yet another knock sounded on the little wooden door.

Knockety-knock-knock-knock!

They all turned to look – and immediately whooped with glee.

Woo-hoo!

How wonderful! What a delight!

Their favourite cousin, with walking stick and lantern, had appeared from nowhere, his little frog peeping out of a dungaree pocket. How did he get to know about the little party?

"Snorrie Magnus!" they all cried at once and a great welcoming, hugging and kissing followed. It had been too long time since this twin-headed adventurer had visited and he was greeted warmly, before all joined hands and danced around the little table in the kitchen, singing merrily as Dotta played her pipes.

After a few minutes, with yet *more* Troll-Cherry Wine poured – a small mug for Snorrie and another for Magnus – Thom raised his hand for silence.

"Mi lovelor frendors," he began solemnly. "Todagen es verisht speshy foor oos."

The trolls, slightly breathless, all nodded and smiled their secret smiles. Finnr looked from one to the other, in puzzlement.

"Todagen," Thom continued, "es verisht speshy foor oor dearig Finnr."

Once more the trolls nodded, eyes twinkling as they nudged each other. Finnr was perplexed. Was it his birthday? He really couldn't remember and, like all trolls, didn't have a clue how old he was. This was all very lovely, being here together with his dear friends and family, but what *was* going on?

Thom raised his troll-mug high and proposed a toast:

"Tvo Finnr, dee Doctoori Troll, en dee speshy nestli homerig! Clinkoori!"

All clinked and chinked their mugs together before taking great slurps of the ruby drink.

"TVO FINNR EN DEE NESTLI HOMERIG!" they shouted. "HIP, HIP – HOORAY!"

Before Finnr could ask any question at all, Thom passed him his weather-stick, plonked his green, floppy hat on his head and ushered him to the open door.

What a sight met his eyes!

A huge array of birds of all shapes, sizes, colours and types flocked to perch on every possible bough and branch of the surrounding trees. There were the fat wood pigeons, pied flycatchers and tree-pipits he knew so well! There were his turtle doves and cuckoos, wood larks and waxwings! There were needletails and woodpeckers and even tawny owls, blinking sleepily, tired from their night-time flights. They tweeted, chirruped, chirped, peeped and twittered. Their songs grew into a cacophonous chorus of salutation which made Finnr's own heart sing along with them. He raised his weather-

177

stick to the sky. Luscinia fluttered to the top and perched prettily. Thom joined the tree-troll.

"Dee tweetors fetchen u, Finnr!" he exclaimed. "U goingor homerig wit dee tweetors."

And so it was. At Luscinia's pretty beckoning, the birds of the forest had come to collect their friend and take him to his new home.

Before Finnr could wave his weather-stick, the birds flew towards him, swooping down to take firm hold. They clutched at his dungarees, his little belt, his braces, his hands, feet, whiskers – anything they could grasp in their little, spiky claws. As one, the bird-cloud rose into the air, lifting Finnr who held on tightly to his green, floppy hat, delight shining in his eyes.

*"...lifting Finnr who held on tightly to his green,
floppy hat..."*

಄

Far away from the forest, where the Big People lived, two miserable figures made their way along the road out of town. One lumbered clumsily. The other scuttled ahead. Each carried suitcases. Neither looked back.

಄

Later in the day, when the sun decided it was time to paint the sky a soft petal pink, before giving way gracefully to a lilac dusk which, in turn, would welcome the twinkle of stars in a mantle of navy blue, a gentle rain began to fall.

As Snorrie Magnus reached the top of his next hill, he looked up.

As Grimhildr and Dotta tucked up their goats for the night, they looked up.

As Hairy Bogley and Ulf prepared their expedition, Herbie Poshtigs waiting and ready, they looked up.

As Hildi and Thom hugged each other in the doorway of their forest cottage, they looked up.

There it was.

In such glorious splendour!

Finnr's weather-stick had created the most beautiful Thank You Rainbow the trolls had ever seen.

Its arc stretched from Mistig Vorter in the fjord below, over the hives of the honey bees, the pear trees, the bilberry bushes and the trees of the forest. It rose over the streams, rivers and lakes. It arched its way into the far distance, over the Great Waterfall's cavern of hidden Troll Treasure, high up to the furthest peak of the mountains and beyond, to other lands; lands and places yet to be discovered and explored.

The sweep of colour embraced the trolls in a crescent of love.

Finnr's rainbow touched them all.